"Beasley elegantly fits together her story's many pieces, crafting a tale where magic is not an illusion but something we can all find . . . A+." —*The Cleveland Plain Dealer*

"Who doesn't love a tale of magic and wonder? *Circus Mirandus* is a gorgeous book." —*Reading Rainbow*

"This lighthearted middle-grade fantasy is an ideal pick for those who want to be immersed in an imaginative world where there is no limit on creativity and adventure." —*VOYA*

"If you enjoy the magical tales of Roald Dahl, you will love this story." —*Kiki* **magazine, Summer Book Club Pick**

"Intriguing . . . At the core of Beasley's debut novel is the theme of eternal life explored in Babbitt's *Tuck Everlasting.*" —*BCCB*

"*Circus Mirandus* is an engaging, innovative tale that balances fantastical goings-on with an exploration of love, loss, friendship and the value of being open to the unexplainable." —*BookPage*

"Cassie Beasley's debut novel is full of mystery, magic, and miraculous events." —*The Christian Science Monitor*

"Beasley's first novel succeeds in tone, suspense, and inventiveness of the magical setting . . . [She] has talent in crafting energy on the page." —*The Horn Book*

"Some books take readers to different places or let us experience fantastical lands, but *Circus Mirandus* brings the magic to our world." —*Scholastic Instructor*, **"50 Best Books for Summer"**

"Beasley has built an imaginative world in evocative, painterly prose, particularly the circus, and she's filled it with compellingly multifaceted characters." —*Booklist*

OTHER BOOKS YOU MAY ENJOY

CIRCUS MIRANDUS

CASSIE BEASLEY

Illustrations by
DIANA SUDYKA

PUFFIN BOOKS

PUFFIN BOOKS
An imprint of Penguin Random House LLC
375 Hudson Street
New York, New York 10014

First published in the United States of America by Dial Books,
an imprint of Penguin Group (USA) LLC, 2015
Published by Puffin Books, an imprint of Penguin Random House LLC, 2016

THE LIBRARY OF CONGRESS HAS CATALOGED THE DIAL BOOKS EDITION AS FOLLOWS:
Beasley, Cassie.
Circus Mirandus / by Cassie Beasley.
pages cm
Summary: "When he realizes that his grandfather's stories of an enchanted circus are true,
Micah Tuttle sets out to find the mysterious Circus Mirandus—and to use its magic to save
his grandfather's life"—Provided by publisher.
ISBN: 978-0-525-42843-5 (hardcover)
[1. Magic—Fiction. 2. Circus—Fiction. 3. Grandfathers—Fiction. 4. Great aunts—Fiction.
5. Orphans—Fiction. 6. Friendship—Fiction. 7. Sick—Fiction.] I. Title.
PZ7.1.B432Cir 2015   [Fic]—dc23   2014031463

Puffin Books ISBN 9780147515544

Printed in the United States of America

9 10

Designed by Jason Henry

For Daddy and Mama. When I was little, you told me
I could do anything. I'm not so little now, but you keep
saying it. I'm starting to think you really believe it.
I love you for that.

· · • · ·

Four small words. That was all it took to set things in motion.

The words came from an upstairs room filled with the rustle of paper and the sweet stink of medicine. They came from the pen of an old man who coughed and wheezed with every breath. They came at the end of a very important letter, which said this:

To: The Lightbender
Care of: Circus Mirandus

I need to speak to you urgently. I hope you remember me even though it's been many years since I was called to Circus Mirandus. Of course I have never forgotten you. My name is Ephraim Tuttle, and we met during the war, when I was a boy.

You promised me a miracle.

I don't know how I will get this message to you. I haven't heard even a whisper about the circus since I was a much younger man. But you made a promise, and I have believed through all these years that if I had need of you, you would come.

Here, the old man paused. He read over what he had written. His pen glinted in the yellow lamplight as he added the final line.

I need you now.

And at that moment, thousands of miles away in the tent of the Man Who Bends Light, a messenger woke up.

2

LIKE A KETTLE

Micah Tuttle knew that most old ladies were pleasant enough. They knitted warm sweaters and baked cakes with chocolate frosting and played old-fashioned card games at the town social hall. Sometimes one forgot to put in her fake teeth, like Mrs. Yolane from the post office, or she kept fourteen kooky cats, like Mrs. Rochester from across the street. But even those two were basically chocolate cakes and warm sweaters on the inside.

Micah's great-aunt, Gertrudis, was not.

He washed a pink china teacup for the third time that Sunday afternoon while she loomed over him. She clucked her tongue, and he scrubbed the cup until he worried the painted roses might fade right off.

On the inside, Aunt Gertrudis was probably cough syrup.

She wore her dust-colored hair twisted into a bun so tight it almost pulled her wrinkled skin smooth, and she starched her shirts until the collars were stiff enough to cut. She made black tea every day in a bright steel kettle. The tea was scalding and bitter, a lot like her, and she wouldn't let Micah add sugar because she said bad teeth ran in the family.

She also said that bad sense ran in the family, and by golly she'd see to it that Micah didn't inherit it.

Aunt Gertrudis had come to stay with them weeks ago, all the way from Arizona, to make sure that things were "done correctly" while Grandpa Ephraim was sick. It wasn't supposed to be for long, but Micah's grandfather had gotten sicker and sicker. And Aunt Gertrudis had gotten more and more impossible.

"Don't assault the cup that way," she snapped at him. "I only wanted you to clean it properly for a change."

The only thing that kept Micah from talking back was the knowledge that she'd keep him up to his elbows in chores for the rest of the day instead of letting him visit with his grandfather. He hadn't been allowed to "pester" Grandpa Ephraim since this morning, when he had hinted that he had something important to tell Micah.

"Something spectacular," his grandfather had whispered. "Something magical."

Grandpa Ephraim had had a sparkle in his eyes that Micah recognized. And *magical* meant Circus Mirandus stories, which were one of Micah's favorite things. Magical also meant Aunt Gertrudis had hustled Micah out of the room before his grandfather could actually tell him anything. She seemed to think that those stories were just the sort of bad sense Micah might inherit if she wasn't careful.

Just a few more minutes until you can see him again.

He passed the teacup to his aunt as politely as he could and went to watch the kettle. While the water heated, the kettle popped like it was stretching out its joints. Soon, the little bird on top would start to whistle. That was Micah's favorite part—the bird singing. He always looked forward to it.

A tendril of steam curled out of the bird's silver mouth. The first faint whistle, when it came, reminded him of the last good days he'd had with Grandpa Ephraim before Aunt Gertrudis had arrived. They'd been building a tree house together. They had worked on it every afternoon, and Grandpa Ephraim had been whistling while they tied knots for the rope ladder. "Tuttle knots!" he'd said when they finished. "You won't find better ones anywhere."

Which, Micah knew, was perfectly true.

Aunt Gertrudis was reaching for the kettle.

"You could leave it," Micah said.

She didn't even glance at him as she jerked the kettle away from the heat. Micah strained his ears, trying to capture the last of the bird's song, but it was too late. All he heard was the *blub glub* of the boiling water inside the kettle, and in an instant, even that sound disappeared.

Aunt Gertrudis sploshed the tea bags up and down.

"It's just that I like to hear it whistle," Micah said quietly.

"It's just that you like to waste time."

Micah stared at the refrigerator so that he wouldn't have to look at her. The things that had once covered the fridge—a recipe for Double Chocolate Brownies, alphabet magnets, a picture of an elephant Micah had drawn when he was seven—had all been papered over with medicine schedules and receipts and Aunt Gertrudis's calorie chart. The only evidence of Micah's existence was a sticky note, half hidden behind a copy of a prescription. It was written in his handwriting, and it said "Inca Project 4 School."

When he had first learned that his grandfather's sister was coming, Micah had hoped she would be as wonderful as Grandpa Ephraim. He had hoped that she would like him. He had thought the house might be less lonely with someone else in it. But it turned out that Aunt Gertrudis didn't like any of the things that Micah's grandfather liked, including ten-year-olds.

He took a deep breath and held it until his chest ached. *Something magical*, he reminded himself. *Maybe a new story. Maybe something happy.*

Happy sounded like someplace very far away and hard to find these day.

Dr. Simon had explained that Grandpa Ephraim couldn't

get enough air. He didn't whistle anymore. He stayed upstairs in bed all day long, and even though he still laughed sometimes, it sounded different. Like the kettle. *Blub glub.*

Micah knew what came next.

3

A LITTLE SPARK

Micah scooped up the tea tray before Aunt Gertrudis could tell him to do it. It was difficult to hold it steady, and the teacups trembled in their saucers as he took a cautious step toward the door.

Aunt Gertrudis blocked his path. "Where do you think you're going?"

Micah tried to smile at her. "Upstairs for tea?"

She gave him a considering look as she lifted the tray out of his hands. "I don't think so," she said. "You're going to sit right here where you won't make a mess."

Micah frowned at her. He didn't make messes. "But I always get to see Grandpa Ephraim during tea."

She sniffed. "Ephraim's been exhausted lately. I think it's best if you don't bother him quite so often."

"But he was feeling better this morning! He wanted to tell me about . . . You just don't want me to talk to him because—"

"Because I don't want you to annoy a very sick man every hour of the day. And because you don't need any more silliness stuffed between your ears, especially not your grandfather's sort of silliness. Now sit." She nodded at the kitchen table.

When he didn't move, she set a pink roses teacup on the table and raised her eyebrow at him.

Lately, Micah felt like he was a rubber band that Aunt Gertrudis was stretching a little farther every time she spoke. Surely it couldn't go on forever. She would have to get tired of pulling eventually. If she didn't, he would snap.

But not today.

Micah dragged his feet as he went to the table, but he went. He gave his aunt the worst glare he could muster.

She turned to the door.

"He'll want to see me," Micah said to her stiff back.

"Drink your tea."

"I think—"

She looked back at him. "Don't you have homework?"

He glanced at the sticky note on the fridge.

"That's what I thought. Maybe you can see Ephraim once you've proven that you are *responsible* and *sensible* about your obligations."

She left without another word.

Micah waited until he could hear the hard soles of her shoes clicking on the stairs, and then he poured his nasty cup of tea down the sink.

When Micah trudged upstairs, Grandpa Ephraim's door was shut tight. Of course. *I'll sneak in as soon as Aunt Gertrudis leaves,* he promised himself.

He went to his room and flopped down on his unmade bed. He *was* supposed to be working on his half of a group project for social studies. Jenny Mendoza, the smartest girl in the whole fifth grade, was expecting Micah to bring a model of an Incan artifact to school tomorrow so that they could rehearse for their presentation. He hadn't exactly started on it yet, but it would be easy. One of the pictures in their textbook was of a thing called a *quipu*, which just looked like a bunch of strings tied into fancy knots, and Micah could do that with his eyes closed. Probably.

Knots weren't regular homework when you were a Tuttle. They were something of a family specialty.

Maybe, thought Micah, *Grandpa Ephraim and I could make the quipu together.* It wasn't as exciting as building a tree house, but it was the sort of project his grandfather might like. Making the quipu together sounded . . . fun, *normal,* like something they would have done before everything went wrong.

Micah rolled off the bed and reached for the bottom drawer of his dresser. A neat coil of blue string lay on top of a nest of odds and ends that he had collected from all over the house when he realized that Aunt Gertrudis's idea of "tidying the place up" meant throwing everything she herself didn't use into the garbage. Micah's socks had had to make room for two yo-yos, a baseball, a felt hat, a small army of action figures, a pack of Old Maid cards, and the string.

He picked it up and wrapped his fingers around it. It was good string, perfect for tying.

All that was left to do was wait.

When he finally heard Aunt Gertrudis shut his grandfather's bedroom door, Micah was out of his room and across the hall in a flash. A sneaky, quiet flash.

He slipped into Grandpa Ephraim's familiar room, and took it all in with a glance. A ceramic duck crouched on top of the alarm clock. A five-gallon pickle jar full of shooter marbles and tarnished coins sat in one corner. Pictures covered the pale blue walls.

A couple of the photos, tucked away in corners, showed his grandfather standing with a pretty young woman who Micah knew was his wife. Grandpa Ephraim didn't like to talk about her. There were pictures of Grandpa Ephraim's friends and places he'd been, and there was even a tiny one of Aunt Gertrudis, taken when she was a little girl. She had a cast on her arm.

Micah liked to look at the pictures of his parents' wedding. They had died in a boating accident when he was four, and the pictures helped him remember them. But his favorite photographs were of him and Grandpa Ephraim together. He liked to think they looked alike, even though his grandfather's hair was gray and his own was brown. Most of the pictures of the two of them were out of focus because they had never figured out how to take a good photo using the timer on the camera. But in every one, they had the same hazel eyes and the same smile.

Grandpa Ephraim didn't look quite like himself these days. His smiles were just as warm as they always had been. But he was thinner, and pale from being stuck in bed all the time. When Micah entered the room, he was propped up on a mound of pillows, staring toward the window. Through the gap in the curtains, Micah could just see the half-finished tree house cradled in the branches of the oak.

"It's a great tree house," said Micah. "It will be a lot of fun this summer. Even without a roof."

Grandpa Ephraim turned to face him. His eyes were bright with secrets. "Oh, there you are, Micah. We have business to discuss, you and I."

"I'm sorry I'm late." Micah made a place for himself on the foot of the bed and set down his coil of blue string. "She kept me away."

"Ah. You missed some delicious tea," Grandpa Ephraim said.

"I bet."

Even though they were both trying to look serious, Grandpa Ephraim's nose wrinkled up at the thought of the inky tea, and Micah's own nose couldn't help itself. They grinned at each other.

"I poured mine down the sink," Micah confessed.

"Well, at least one of us escaped!" Grandpa Ephraim said.

That was true enough. But Micah would drink a whole kettle of ink every day if it meant they could spend more time together.

"I . . . why is Aunt Gertrudis always so . . . the way she is?" He didn't want to tell Grandpa Ephraim that his sister was *horrible*, but it was hard not to complain sometimes.

Grandpa Ephraim sighed. "Your great-aunt and I haven't been close for a very long time. It's my fault as much as it is hers."

"I doubt that," Micah muttered.

His grandfather raised an eyebrow. "It was good of her to come. She's not happy here, but we do need the help."

I could do everything she does, Micah thought. *And I would be a lot nicer about doing it.*

"I know she can be frustrating. If you could just try to get along with her for a little while longer—"

"I *am* trying." He didn't know how to explain it, to say that it seemed like he was doing nothing but trying these days. He was trying not to upset Aunt Gertrudis, and he was trying to find ways to help his grandfather, and he was trying to be okay even though he was pretty sure he wasn't. "I'm trying a lot."

"I know you are. And you're doing wonderfully, Micah. You really are." He looked toward the window again. "I need to tell you something."

Micah smiled. "Something magical? I was hoping it would be one of your Circus Mirandus stories."

Their eyes met, and Micah felt something pass between them. A zing, a little spark of knowing that whatever his grandfather was about to say would change everything.

"I've written a letter to an old friend," said Grandpa Ephraim. "I think you should read it."

IMPOSSIBLE LETTERS

Grandpa Ephraim opened the drawer of his bed-side table to reveal balls of crumpled paper. Micah uncrumpled them one by one until the bed was covered with letters, letters made up of impossible words.

Lightbender, the letters said.

Circus Mirandus, they said.

And they said one more thing, one very crucial thing. *You promised me a miracle.*

Micah knew about the promise the Lightbender had made to his grandfather. It came at the very end of the story, and it was one of Micah's favorite parts. But . . . it was only a story.

His grandfather placed his hand on top of one of the crinkled sheets of paper. "It took me quite a few drafts to get it right."

"I don't understand," said Micah. "Circus Mirandus isn't—"

"Real?" Grandpa Ephraim said quietly. "But it is."

A smile was tugging up every wrinkle of Grandpa Ephraim's face. It wasn't a teasing smile.

Micah stared at all of the letters spread across the crocheted blanket. "If it's really true . . ."

Grandpa Ephraim laughed his *blub glub* laugh and beckoned with one arm. When Micah reached for him, he pulled him close in a weak hug and wheezed in his ear, "It's the truest thing ever. I'm so sorry I never told you."

Micah hadn't realized there was a fist in his chest until his grandfather's words made it unclench. Grandpa Ephraim would never lie about something so important. And that meant . . . that meant magic was real. And, more importantly, a real magician had made a promise to his grandfather. Micah wouldn't have to be alone. The Lightbender could save Grandpa Ephraim. The world would go back to being the way it was supposed to be.

Micah hugged his grandfather so tightly that his arms hurt. "Everything's going to be all right," he said. "It is."

Grandpa Ephraim lay back on his pillows and nodded. "I think it might. I finished the final draft of the letter last night, and a messenger came for it."

"What?"

"It was the most astonishing thing. I wish you could have been here to see it. I had no idea how to get the letter to the circus, but the messenger flew in through the window a few hours after I had finished writing it."

"Wait. Did you say flew?"

Grandpa Ephraim's grin widened. "Yes. It does sound strange, doesn't it? Apparently the Lightbender uses a parrot for his mail. She said she preferred to take phone calls, actually, but I'm really not sure how that would work. I should have expected something fantastic."

"Phone calls?" Micah rubbed at the back of his neck with one hand. "This . . . it's so . . . wow!"

He looked around the bedroom and realized that everything had been transformed. This wasn't a room where Grandpa Ephraim had been sick; it was a room where he was going to get well again. Even the afternoon sunbeams that shone through the window seemed brighter.

"And this mail parrot—she was going to give the Lightbender your message? She was going to tell him to come here?"

"Yes," Grandpa Ephraim said. He bent over and coughed a couple of times. Micah started to pass him a tissue from the box on the bedside table, but he waved it away. "I hope," he said, "that he'll agree to help us."

"He has to." If this was real—and it just had to be— then the Lightbender would help them. Micah didn't see how he could refuse. In Grandpa Ephraim's story he was a very powerful magician, a *good* magician, and he had promised.

"I can't wait for you to meet him." Grandpa Ephraim coughed again. "The messenger said Circus Mirandus was in La Paz right now."

"Where—"

"It's in Bolivia. So I'm not sure how—" *Blub glub.*

Micah handed him a tissue, and this time he coughed into it.

"Do you think it will take long?" Micah asked. "For the Lightbender to fix you, I mean."

Aunt Gertrudis would have to move out of the spare bedroom to make room for their guest, he decided. She would be glad to be going back to Arizona without Micah anyway. She'd been saying just the other day how difficult it would be to find room for him in her apartment.

"What?" Grandpa Ephraim was coughing so hard that he barely got the word out.

"Are you okay?"

Blub glub. "I think I need . . ." Grandpa Ephraim's face was turning pale. His eyes were clenched shut. His mouth was opening and closing like a fish's, and all of his words had turned into nothing but *blub glub*, *blub glub*.

Micah was on his feet in an instant. "Grandpa? What should I do?"

That awful, dying-kettle sound was lasting for much too long. He was about to ask if he should fetch a cup of water, or the breathing machine that the doctor had given them, but hands were on his shoulders, jerking him away.

Aunt Gertrudis's nostrils flared. "Out!" she said. "Get out. Getting him excited for no good reason."

Her eyes landed on the letters spread out on the bed. They narrowed into slits.

"This again," she hissed. "I should have known."

Micah didn't know what possessed him in that moment, but it was something with a lot of bravery and almost no good sense. Instead of leaving, he ducked around his aunt and made a wild grab for the letters.

He managed to snag one of them before Aunt Gertrudis caught him by the back of his T-shirt. "I said *out!*" she shouted. "Go to your room!"

She snatched at the letter in his hand as she shoved him toward the door. Micah's fist was closed too tightly around the paper, though. It ripped, and he stumbled out into the hall, nearly colliding with the wall. The door slammed behind him, and the lock clicked.

"Grandpa Ephraim!" he yelled. "Are you all right? Aunt Gertrudis? Please let me in!"

Nobody answered.

Micah slid down the wall and sat, staring at the door, wishing that it would burst into a thousand splinters. The silence from the other side seemed to last forever before he heard the breathing machine turn on. The grinding sound of it made him feel like he might never be able to move from that spot again.

The half of the letter that he had managed to rescue

from Grandpa Ephraim's room trembled in his hands. Micah pressed the creases out as best he could, running his fingers across the words over and over again until the paper began to feel soft.

You have to get up, he told himself.

He had to be ready to meet the Lightbender when he came. He had to make sure that Grandpa Ephraim got his miracle before it was too late.

5
THE MESSENGER

The messenger's name was Chintzy, and she returned to Circus Mirandus just before the sun set on a dreary afternoon. She ignored the excited *oohs* and *aahs* of the children who spotted her as she zipped toward the black-and-gold tent she called home.

"All this rain!" she squawked once she was safely atop her perch. "I don't know why the Head allows it. Gray, cold, *wet*. Ruins the mood of the place."

She ruffled her damp red feathers and glared with one beady yellow eye at the Man Who Bends Light, who was fiddling with an ornate silver coffee service beside her perch. He looked as he had for centuries. His sandy hair was a tangled nest, and his beaten, brown leather coat swept the ground. His nose was strong—almost, Chintzy had been known to admit from time to time, like a proper beak.

"The meadow around the circus needs rain as much as any other living thing," he said. "You're just in a snit because you wasted your day on a fool's errand. Not every twitch of your tail is a magical event. I told you I wasn't expecting any messages."

Chintzy snatched a lemon cookie off the coffee tray with one clawed foot. "Shows what you know," she muttered around a beakful of crumbs.

"I told you," he said again, then paused. "Wait. There was a message?"

She shook her tail feathers at him. "You won't be insulting my tail twitches anymore, will you?" she said smugly. "I wouldn't have gone if there wasn't a message. Flying all that way. My poor wings!"

The tray rattled as he plunked the creamer onto it. "Who could possibly . . .?" He looked sharply at her. "It wasn't Victoria. Was it?"

Chintzy honk-snorted at him. It was her favorite rude sound. "Of course not! After all these years? Not that I would deliver a message for *her* anyway. Not after what she did."

"I suppose that is for the best. Who sent the message?"

"You suppose right. Can you imagine what the Head would say?"

"The message, Chintzy," he reminded her.

"I almost perished of fatigue, you know." She drooped on her perch in an attempt to look terribly forlorn and dramatic. "You could have lost me."

He rolled his eyes. "I am rarely so lucky."

Chintzy shrieked.

"Do not *swear* at me. I know for a fact that Porter opened a Door for you last night. It's not as though you had to flap all the way there."

She turned her back on him. "Ingrate."

He sighed. "I know. I am sorry, Chintzy. I do appreciate your hard work. Would you please give me the message?"

"Well, if you're going to beg . . ." She spun around and puffed out her scarlet chest. "I'm a professional, you know. The letter disintegrated in this rain you insist upon defending, but I memorized it for safekeeping."

"Very impressive."

"I am," she agreed. "The message is from a child who saw your show."

Then she paused and tilted her head. "Well, no, that's not exactly right. He's not a child anymore. He grew up."

The Man Who Bends Light furrowed his brow. "It's from an adult?"

"He almost shocked the eggs out of me," Chintzy admitted. "It's that serious. You're going to be in such trouble with the Head, and . . . well, I guess I'll let you hear it." She cleared her throat to acknowledge the formality of the situation, and then she recited Ephraim's letter.

After she finished, the tent was silent for a long time.

The Man Who Bends Light stood as still as a petrified stump. As the minutes dragged by, the quiet started to itch. Chintzy plucked a couple of particularly beautiful chest feathers before she even realized how nervous she was.

She cleared her throat again. "He shortened your name, such as it is. *Lightbender.* Clever. Much more modern."

When he didn't respond, she bobbed her head and added, "He called me *ma'am*, too. You should take notes."

"As if your ego needed stroking." He folded his legs and sank onto a tasseled floor cushion. "Ephraim Tuttle," he murmured. "That is something I didn't expect."

"Who is he? Looked about as special as a goose on a pond, if you ask me. Not the sort we usually deal with."

The Man Who Bends Light looked thoughtful. "He is a child who was called to Circus Mirandus. Or he was. And he was special, compared to most." He stared down at his long fingers, and a smile crept across his lips. "He showed me a magic trick."

"A real one?"

"Quite." He glanced at her. "Do you know what Ephraim wants for his miracle?"

"I'm not sure. He wants to talk to you. Maybe . . ." Chintzy refused to look at him.

"What is it?"

"He's very old," she said. "And he's dying, I think."

The Man Who Bends Light flinched. "Dying? What if he wants something impossible?"

"Well, that's a problem for you, isn't it?" Chintzy turned

her head around to preen a few feathers that had been mussed by the rain. "I didn't even know the children *could* save their miracles. Never heard of that before."

"Nobody before Ephraim ever asked to. I didn't expect him to wait so long. I had almost forgotten." He was pacing now, back and forth in front of Chintzy's perch. "I'll have to speak to Mr. Head."

"He'll feed you to one of his creatures," she predicted.

"Nevertheless." He strode toward the curtain that served as a door. "Go back to Ephraim. Find out exactly what he needs. I must be prepared."

"What do you mean 'go back'? I just got home!"

"Back," he said. "Talk to Porter about a Door."

Chintzy fluffed herself to threatening proportions. "I'm *not* your carrier pigeon."

"Go."

The word echoed between them. Chintzy hated it when he used that voice, that deep tone with his magic bleeding through at the edges. She ground her beak.

"Fine!" she squawked. "I don't know how you got into this mess anyway. Thought you didn't offer miracles."

"I did once," he said softly. The lamps in the tent seemed to dim for a moment. "Before."

6

EPHRAIM'S BEACH

There were doors, and then there were Doors. They were exactly the same thing, except one kind of door led from, say, the living room to the kitchen, and the other covered considerably more distance. Porter was Circus Mirandus's expert on the latter, and it was thanks to him they could travel so quickly when they had need.

If Chintzy had only asked nicely, Porter could have opened a Door much closer to her destination. But, stubborn bird that she was, she didn't ask Porter nicely. In fact, she was in such an unfortunate mood that she bit him on the chin. So instead of enjoying a short flight to the Tuttle house, she found herself flapping around in the city's sewer system. She dodged dead goldfish and slime as she looked for a way out, and all the while she wondered: What on earth was so special about Ephraim Tuttle?

When Ephraim Tuttle was a boy, ten years old to be precise, his father was fighting in the war overseas.

Corporal Tuttle fought in the war all day long and often all night long and sometimes even in the spaces between day and night that most people were too lazy to recognize properly. At home, Ephraim's mother spent just as much time at her own job. She had a beautiful smile and a voice like a foghorn, and as best as her son could tell, her job during those dark days involved bellowing encouraging things to young men who were leaving on the big ships to fight in the war themselves.

Obviously, Ephraim's parents were very important people. Both of them being vital to the effort, he was left with a lot of free time on his hands.

Now, adults might not know this, but ten is a difficult age. Especially if there is a war going on and if your parents leave you to your own devices too much.

Ephraim did not like school, so he didn't go very often. He had better things to do. Every morning he put on a clever-looking felt hat that belonged to his father, and he tipped it back so that it wouldn't fall down over his eyes. And, imagining he looked quite grown-up, he took himself to the beach.

Ephraim's beach was not a sunny, tropical beach. It was the kind of beach that has little sun and lots of fog and pebbles instead of sand. To make matters worse, the water was dark gray most days, and it was usually too cold for swimming. The sounds were very unbeach-like as well. The waves swished, the pebbles clacked, and his mother's voice, all the way from the port, sometimes echoed out of the fog, crying, "Farewell, boys. Our prayers go with you."

The whole affair smelled like oily fish and algae.

Now, Ephraim was fairly normal, for a ten-year-old with too much free time. He liked sunshine and penny candy and warm beaches with yellow sand. But his beach was as close as he could get to the war overseas, so it was as close as he could get to his father. And that, of course, was important.

Ephraim always took paper and pencils with him to the beach, and he would sit with his back to a mossy rock and write letters to his father.

Letters that said things like this:

> *Dear Father,*
>   *I hope you are doing very well in the war and that you are safe and that you will come home with a lot of awards for being the bravest father in the entire world.*
>   *I am not at school today because the smallest toe on my left foot hurts. I am at the*

beach, and Mother's voice sounds lonely. I
think you had better come home very soon.
All my love,
Ephraim

And like this:

Dear Father,
Mother told me that I had to go to school
today, and I told her that I would. But I
am at the beach again, tossing pebbles at the
gulls.
I think you had better come home very
soon because I am considering becoming a
train robber.
All my love,
Ephraim

And also like this:

Dear Father,
I am never going to school until you come
back home. I told Mother, and I think it
made her cry. I apologized and told her I
didn't mean it.
But I did. And soon I will have to become
a train robber because I will be so far behind

at arithmetic and geography and penmanship
that no decent job will have me.
    Unless you come home, of course. In which
case I will be a famous archaeologist.
All my love,
Ephraim

He meant every word.

For his part, Ephraim's father had managed to send only one letter back across the water to his wife and son. It was short.

My dear family,
    I am sorry to be away from you, and I
pray for your safety and happiness every day.
I am sorry I can't be there to help you and
hold you.
    But I am not sorry to be here, because
today I tied a knot that kept a boy not much
older than Ephraim from dying, and that is
worth something. Don't worry, Ephraim,
I'll teach it to you when I get home.
Until my next letter,
O. Tuttle

Ephraim read this letter until he wore holes in the paper. He kept trying to make it longer by looking for mysterious codes and secret messages, but only two parts might have been mysterious even to a stranger. One was the *O*, which stood for Obadiah, and the other was the line about knots, which were his father's favorite hobby.

Ephraim supposed that his father was too busy tying knots and saving boys, who were almost himself but not quite, to get around to writing a second letter. That didn't stop him from writing his own. Even though, after such a long time, he didn't entirely believe that his father would receive them.

Ephraim wrote a lot of letters because during the war there were a lot of days.

Ephraim was at the beach when the wind changed. It was midmorning, and he had spent a pleasant hour scraping together moss from the rocks and some frail twigs in order to build a small, mossy soldier with a thin, twiggy gun. He was thinking he might dry this little soldier out and mail him to his father for luck, when it happened.

One moment, the wind was coming from the land, whipping Ephraim's hair around his temples and chilling his ankles where the pants he'd outgrown no longer met his boots. Then it stopped.

For an instant, everything was impossibly still.

Ephraim had just enough time to realize something unusual was going on, just enough time to blink, before the wind started blowing again in a new direction. It blew in from the ocean, and it blew harder than any wind he'd ever felt before, so hard that he stumbled backward toward the dunes. He leaned against the wind until he was certain he wouldn't fall, then he squinted his eyes and looked around.

The long grass of the dunes tossed its brown seed heads. The smallest pebbles, the ones that were almost sand, skittered across the beach. But the surface of the sea was flat, as though the great wind were God's iron, smoothing every ripple and crease from the fabric of the ocean. The gray water was so smooth that it looked, for all the world, like a sheet of the finest window glass. Ephraim picked up a pebble and tossed it toward the water, and it disappeared without a splash.

It's important, when you first see magic, to recognize it. You don't often get a second chance. Ephraim knew that what he was seeing was magic straightaway, but he misunderstood its purpose.

I must surely be able to walk, he thought, *across a sea so very flat. I must be able to walk all the way to Europe and to the war and to my father.*

He promptly set about trying, and he was just as promptly disappointed. When he pushed his way to the edge of the beach, Ephraim's feet sank into the water, which was as wet and cold as it ever had been. And while he was trying to free himself from the sucking ocean floor, he got soaked all the way up to his armpits.

He also got a fish stuck in his left boot.

The boot had always fit loosely, and as it filled up with

seawater, a tiny silver fish, smaller than Ephraim's pinkie finger, decided to take up residence next to his ankle.

It was a ticklish and embarrassing situation, but before he could do anything to remedy it, Ephraim heard the music. Not classical music, not choir music, not even the dire wails of a hurdy-gurdy. The music that calls a person to magic is always the same.

Pipes and drums.

From somewhere beyond the dunes, the pipes skirled and the drums thrummed, and Ephraim followed them. He followed them as countless children before him had followed, as some few lucky ones still do.

7

JENNY MENDOZA

Even when your whole world was off balance, you still woke up in the morning to find there were a hundred perfectly ordinary things to do. For example, Micah's grandfather was very ill and Micah had just been told that magic was real, but he still had to get dressed and brush his teeth. He still had to choke down a bowl full of Aunt Gertrudis's favorite fiber cereal for breakfast. And, because his great-aunt was not nearly as distracted as Ephraim's mother had been during that terrible war, Micah had to go to school.

He stood in the front hall, the toes of his sneakers just touching the edge of the living room carpet. Aunt Gertrudis sat on the sofa with her back turned toward him, staring at the television. The local weatherman was talking about what a pleasant April the town of Peal was having that year.

"Not a drop of rain last week," he said. "The Recreation Department couldn't have asked for a better grand opening of the new downtown facility."

"You locked Grandpa Ephraim's door."

"I know."

"Can I at least go talk to him?" Micah asked. "I want to say good-bye."

Aunt Gertrudis didn't look away from the television. "Brush your hair, Micah. You'll be late for the bus."

Micah's hair never tangled. He didn't even own a hairbrush, but Aunt Gertrudis refused to believe that. "Please! I just want to make sure he's all right."

She finally turned around. "He's resting. I called Doctor Simon and we've agreed to increase the dosage on some of his medicines now that he doesn't have much time left. That will make him sleep more."

"Doesn't have much time left." The words didn't sound right coming out of Micah's mouth. They were muffled and flat, like he was trying to talk with a pillow shoved against his face.

"Yes." Her lips puckered to one side. "You *knew* this was going to happen. I won't have you bothering him in his final days."

Micah didn't repeat "final days." He couldn't take a deep enough breath because of the invisible pillow.

His aunt turned back to the television. "And I won't

have him destroying what little sense you have with that ridiculous story. I saw those scraps of paper all over the room. Ephraim can't let that old joke go.

"A magical circus," she huffed. "I hope you know he's making fun of you."

Micah shook his head, then realized she couldn't see him with her face turned toward the weatherman. "No," he said quietly. "You're wrong."

"What's that?" Aunt Gertrudis asked, but Micah knew from the sharpness in her voice that she had heard him.

A few minutes later, Micah stood by himself at the school bus stop. *She's wrong, wrong, wrong,* he thought. The Lightbender *would* come, very soon Micah hoped, and he would fix Grandpa Ephraim. Everything would go back to the way it was supposed to be.

But what if something went wrong? Micah had hardly slept last night, imagining all of the terrible things that might happen.

The Lightbender might not come in time. If he did come in time, Aunt Gertrudis might not let him in the house. Or maybe he would send his parrot messenger back and tell Grandpa Ephraim that he had to come to Bolivia to get the miracle. But after yesterday, Micah was sure his grandfather was too sick to get out of bed. What would Micah do then?

I would go to Bolivia for Grandpa Ephraim and explain everything to the Lightbender, he thought. *I would make him come back with me.*

He didn't know how he would do this, but he thought it enough times so that when Florence Greeber showed up to wait for the bus, Micah was half convinced that going to Bolivia would be a lot like taking a trip to the other side of the city. Only it would take longer, and you would have to change airplanes instead of buses.

He was feeling almost calm and even a little happy until he saw what Florence was carrying. Florence was the only other fifth grader at Peal Elementary School who rode the bus with Micah, and when she staggered up to the stop, her red curls were barely visible behind the enormous model of an Egyptian pyramid that she was holding in both of her arms.

"Hey." Florence's voice came from behind the pyramid.

The model was fantastic. Florence had even made statues out of clay to guard the pyramid's entrance.

"My partner's bringing paint so that we can do hieroglyphics today during group work, and then it will be done," she said. "What do you think?"

Micah thought he should probably run away from the bus stop as fast as possible.

He'd completely forgotten he was supposed to be bringing an Incan artifact to school today. He'd left his quipu string in his grandfather's room, which might as well have been the moon with the way his aunt was behaving.

Maybe Mrs. Stark would think he'd gotten sick over the weekend. Jenny Mendoza was the smartest girl in class; she could probably finish the whole project by herself. She could probably do a better job without Micah's help.

"It's good, isn't it?" said Florence.

"It's great," Micah squeaked.

Florence stretched her head up over the tip of the pyramid. She squinted at his backpack, like she was trying to figure out if he had somehow stuffed an amazing project in it.

What was he going to tell Jenny? They were supposed to be finishing their artifact today so that they could give their presentation tomorrow. She might tell Mrs. Stark that Micah hadn't done his part, and then Mrs. Stark would call Aunt Gertrudis.

That would be . . . not good at all.

When the bus came, Florence kicked Micah in the leg to get his attention. "What's *wrong* with you today? Help me get this thing on the bus."

She yelped when he tried to take the pyramid out of her hands, so he dragged her bag up the bus steps for her instead.

Florence tottered to the back, and Micah waited while she set the model up in its own seat and brushed a speck of lint off one of her miniature statues. "I figure everyone else is going to do something small," she told Micah. "Mine's going to be the best. Don't you think so?"

Normally, Micah wouldn't have thought so. On any other day, he would have thought that Jenny Mendoza and her partner would have the best project. But since *he* was Jenny's partner, he nodded at Florence and wished that the driver would forget the way to Peal Elementary.

The first thing Micah did when he got to school was check the arts and crafts closet in the back of the classroom for something, *anything*, that he might be able to use for his project. After some digging, he found a ball of yarn that nobody had ever used because it was an awful snotty color. He took it back to his desk and set to work.

Or at least he tried to.

He found the picture of the quipu in his book. The caption said the long string of knots was an ancient method of record keeping. The knots represented numbers and maybe even words, so that an Incan could tell all kinds of things just by looking at them, like how many llamas had been sold last year. Micah thought this was a fascinating idea. Unfortunately, it wasn't exactly easy to re-create while he was hiding his hands under his desk so that Mrs. Stark wouldn't see.

He decided he would tie twenty-four different knots, one for each student in the class. Mrs. Stark might think that was a nice thing to do.

Jenny caught Micah's eye from across the room during the Pledge of Allegiance. She bounced on the balls of her feet and waved at him. He tried to smile back, but it was hard to make his lips move in the right direction.

She didn't seem to notice. She grinned even wider and

pointed toward a thick stack of papers on the corner of her desk.

"The report," she mouthed.

A couple of the girls in the row behind Jenny giggled into their hands, and one of them waved exaggeratedly at Micah and then rolled her eyes.

Did they always make fun of Jenny? She was the newest student in their class. Micah knew she was smart, but he hadn't paid much attention to her otherwise. He had just assumed that she had a lot of friends because it seemed like everyone else did. It would be awful if people were cruel to her because Micah ruined their project. He started tying as soon as he sat back down.

It should have been easy. Grandpa Ephraim liked to say that Tuttles and knots went together like toast and cheese, and Micah had always been proud of how easily knot tying came to him. But for some reason, his fingers wouldn't work the way he wanted them to today.

He tried to tie a knot to represent Nathan Borgle, who sat at the desk in front of him. Nathan was tall and he had a chipped tooth. He was always in trouble for something. A Nathan Borgle knot would be big and sturdy and not too good-looking. Micah knew hundreds of knots, but when he tried to tie Nathan into the snot-colored yarn, all he got was a tangle.

Come on, come on, he thought.

If Mrs. Stark called Aunt Gertrudis and told her Micah wasn't doing his work . . . well, what if she did something that kept him from helping his grandfather? He yanked on the yarn, looped it, pinched it, and finally, after what seemed like ages, he had a knot.

A knot that was not anything like Nathan Borgle.

Micah waited until nobody was looking in his direction, and then he stared down at his hands. The knot was soft and smooth. It was almost as big as Micah's thumbnail. And though it felt warm against his fingers, the edges of it were beginning to fray.

Micah swallowed hard. This was a knot unlike any other, but it wasn't what he'd been trying to make. When he closed his hand around it, it didn't feel like any of the regular knots he knew. It didn't feel like an ancient artifact. Somehow, it felt like a *person*, and not one of Micah's classmates.

It felt like Grandpa Ephraim. Warm and wonderful and coughing and wheezing and slowly, oh so slowly, coming undone.

Micah stared up at the board. It swam in front of his eyes while he held the knot that was somehow just like his grandfather close to his stomach.

He picked up the yarn and tried again. And again. He tied a dozen knots that were supposed to represent his classmates while Mrs. Stark wrote math problems on the board.

He tied his grandfather a dozen times.

Just before lunchtime, everyone swapped desks so that they would be sitting next to their partners.

Micah sank in his seat and tried not to see the different artifacts appearing from backpacks and cubbies, but they were impossible to ignore. Florence's model was obviously the best. Nathan had brought a boomerang. Several other students had made papier-mâché masks. Some of the projects were kind of weird-looking, and Giles Darby had obviously sat on his miniature cardboard chariot. But every pair had *something*.

Jenny trotted over with her stack of paper in hand. "Hi!" she said. "I've got everything we need."

She turned an empty desk to face Micah and plopped down. He had just enough time to see that every page of her report had been color-coded with markers before she said, "Stop me if I say anything you don't agree with," and launched into the speech she'd written for them.

Micah should have interrupted her right away. The longer Jenny talked, the more he wanted to crawl under the desk and vanish. Jenny had come up with discussion questions and made lists of fun facts to share with the class. It was going to be the best presentation in the whole fifth grade, definitely, except for the fact that Micah hadn't done his part.

"So that's that," Jenny finished breathlessly. She beamed at him. "I can add in anything you want about our artifact."

Then she looked across the tops of the desks between them. She blinked. "Our artifact," she said. "What did you bring?"

For one wild moment, Micah imagined running over to

Florence Greeber and stealing her pyramid and giving it to Jenny. But he was pretty sure Florence would smash him. She and her partner were bending over it with tiny paintbrushes in their hands.

"I'm really sorry, Jenny," he said.

"What for?"

Micah gulped. He saw realization steal the smile from her face. Her brown eyes got wide, her lips pursed like she wanted to spit but couldn't because her manners were too good for that.

"I don't . . . I don't understand," she said. She started twisting one of her two black braids around her fingers nervously. "We discussed this together on Friday. You agreed that you would make the model if I did the report!"

"I know."

"I don't understand!" she said again. Micah could tell by the shrillness in her voice that she really didn't. "It's due *tomorrow*."

Micah didn't know what to say. Jenny was yanking on her braid now. He took a deep breath and pulled his handful of knotted yarn out of the desk where he'd stuffed it. He pushed it toward her without looking at it.

"Oh," said Jenny. "It's a quipu. Sort of."

He was surprised that she could tell. Someone who had had this desk before Micah had gouged a sharp letter *V* into the corner of it. He had never noticed it before, but now he stared at it so that he wouldn't have to face Jenny or the knots.

"It's not a bad idea. Only the one in the book was, you know, a lot bigger." She sounded like she was trying very hard to be positive. Out of the corner of his eye, he saw her pick at one of the knots with her bitten fingernails. "And there were different colored strings," she said. "And, well, these knots are all . . ."

"Grandpa Ephraim," he whispered.

". . . the same." Jenny dug another fingernail into the knot, as though she were going to pry it apart.

Micah flung out his arm and snatched the string of knots from her hands so quickly that Jenny yelped.

"Hey!" She rubbed her hands together.

Micah's face felt hot. "I'm sorry, okay?" he muttered. "I'll fix it tonight. I'll make it better."

"You can't make me do all the work," said Jenny. "It's not fair."

"I'll fix it. I promise." He tucked the yarn carefully into the front pocket of his backpack.

"I hope so," she said. "It doesn't look much like an artifact right now. There's something funny about those knots."

Micah felt like she'd punched him on the nose. "It's not *funny.*"

Her brows drew together. "Are you all right?"

Micah wasn't. He was shaking, and he felt hot all over now. "It's not funny," he said. "He's dying."

THE WHOLE,
PLAIN TRUTH

Jenny's eyes widened.

"I mean he's . . ." Micah choked. What was wrong with him? Why had he said that? "I mean he's sick. He's very sick."

"Oh," Jenny said quietly. She leaned toward him.

He leaned away. "It's fine, okay. I'm sorry about the project. I didn't mean to say he was . . . he's just been sick. I can finish the quipu tonight." He couldn't stop babbling.

"Micah?" Jenny sounded worried.

He shook his head at her. He didn't want to hear whatever she was going to say. "I'm fine. Completely fine."

But his throat was tight, and his eyes stung, and he couldn't do *this*. Not here. Not in front of everybody.

It's just a stupid project. It's just homework. He's not dying. You can't cry like a little kid in the middle of class.

Jenny jumped to her feet. "The supply closet!" she hissed.

"What?" Micah croaked.

But Jenny was already pulling him out of his seat and top-speeding him toward the back of the classroom.

The craft closet was tiny and dark, and it smelled like glue. Jenny and Micah barely fit. Something that was probably an elbow hit him in the chin before Jenny managed to pull the chain that turned on the single lightbulb.

"I don't think we're supposed to be in here together," Micah whispered.

"Are you okay?" She was still twisting one of her braids around her finger. Her eyes were filled with worry. "This is a good place for . . . I thought you were going to cry."

"I *wasn't.*"

"I didn't mean to hurt your feelings," she said. "What . . . ?"

She trailed off. Micah knew by the way her lips pressed together that she was bottling up a hundred questions. He braced himself. She was going to ask him why his half of their project was a mess and who was sick and other painful things. He wasn't sure he could stand it.

But after a moment, Jenny said, "Never mind."

Micah blinked at her.

She dropped her braid and clasped her hands in front of

her skirt. "I'll finish the project if you need me to. I'll tell Mrs. Stark you helped."

Maybe it was because Jenny *hadn't* asked, or maybe it was because she was the kind of person who knew that the craft supply closet was a good place to hide when you were about to cry. Whatever the reason, Micah found himself telling her the truth.

"It's my grandfather who's sick. I didn't mean to forget about the presentation."

Once he'd told her that much, Micah didn't quite know how to stop. Jenny didn't interrupt while he talked about Grandpa Ephraim and Aunt Gertrudis and the horrible sound of the breathing machine. Everything came out of him in a rush, like he was a punctured balloon.

He even told her about Circus Mirandus and the miracle.

Jenny didn't say anything at first, and Micah became uncomfortably aware of the fact that he was standing beside a box full of Christmas tinsel, pouring his secret thoughts out to someone he barely knew. He could hear his classmates talking just feet away, their voices garbled through the door.

"I'm so sorry," Jenny said quietly. She sounded like she really meant it. "About your grandfather and your aunt. That's horrible."

Micah opened his mouth to say that it was all right. But it wasn't. Instead, he reached into his back pocket and pulled out the ripped copy of the letter he'd taken from Grandpa Ephraim's room the night before.

Jenny leaned back against a shelf full of pipe cleaners and read it. "The Lightbender," she said. "I guess that's a stage name?"

Micah shrugged. "I don't think he has another one."

"I don't mean to be rude, but . . . wouldn't he be dead by now? If your grandfather met him when he was a boy?"

"Of course not."

"What?"

"It's a magical circus," Micah explained. "He's lived a very long time."

It was only after Jenny started to shift uncomfortably from foot to foot that Micah realized how strange a phrase like "magical circus" sounded at school.

"You don't believe me." Of course she didn't. She probably thought he was crazy.

Jenny shook her head. "I don't think you're a liar."

Her smile looked nervous to Micah.

"It's just . . ." she said. "Well, I think you might have mis-understood what your grandfather was trying to tell you."

He fought down the urge to snap at her. "I didn't."

Jenny stared with narrowed eyes at a spot a few inches above his head. After a minute, she said, "I really will finish the project. You won't get in trouble that way. You should spend as much time as you can with him."

"I can't let you do that," Micah said automatically.

But he wasn't sure he *could* finish it. After the way the knots had behaved today, he wasn't sure about anything. "I can . . . I'll try to make it up to you somehow."

She shook her head. "When my grandmother found out she was dying a couple of years ago, she told us she was going back to Mexico. To her hometown. She wanted to see it one last time. My dad—well, he didn't approve. He told her she was too old to make a trip like that, but she sold her house and her car and she *went*. She called me when she got there, and she sounded so happy."

"Um . . ."

"I was proud of her," Jenny explained. "She got her dying wish. Things like that are important. It sounds like your grandfather's dying wish is to see this Lightbender person one last time."

Micah nodded. "For his miracle. The Lightbender can make him better again."

Jenny bit her lip. "Micah? You know magic isn't real. Right?"

Micah opened his mouth to say that of course he knew that. He didn't believe in dragons or leprechauns or witches. Those were just fairy tales. But Circus Mirandus was different. The Lightbender was different.

Before he could say any of these things, though, Jenny was talking again. "Your grandfather . . . maybe he just embellished the real story. Maybe there really was a circus, and it was special to him. That's why he wrote the letter. Now that he's sick, he's trying to find the circus again."

"He didn't *embellish*." Grandpa Ephraim had told the whole, plain truth.

"Oh, of course he did!" Jenny cried.

She glanced at the door and lowered her voice. "He was trying to make the story more fun for you. He was trying to make it exciting and special. That's what grown-ups do when they tell stories to children!"

Micah tried to take a step back, but there was no room. He shook his head. "You don't understand."

Jenny's face scrunched with sympathy, and Micah jerked his eyes away. What was he thinking? That a brainy girl like Jenny Mendoza would believe in magicians and miracles? Just because she had been nice about the project . . .

He shouldn't have told her. He should have known better.

"Micah—"

She was interrupted by the door swinging open. The sound of their classmates' chatter filled the closet.

Florence stood in the doorway. "What are you two doing in here?" she asked suspiciously.

"Nothing," Jenny and Micah said at the same time.

"Well, I need some glue, so . . ."

"Here." Jenny thrust a bottle of X-tra Strong Craft Paste at her. "We were having a private conversation about our project."

"No we weren't," said Micah. He pushed past Florence and headed for his desk.

"Micah, wait a minute!" Jenny called.

He pretended not to hear her.

9
THE FIGHT

Aunt Gertrudis was in the living room when Micah came home from school that day. She was on the house phone with one of her Arizona friends, and she was talking about joining an aquarobics class that would be starting at her health club there in two weeks.

Micah knew it would be best to ignore her. He just wanted to check on his grandfather, and she hated to be interrupted when she was on the phone. But as he headed for the stairs she said, "Of course I'll be back by then, Harriet. This thing can't drag on forever, and I've already got everything sorted out here. I'll be on the way home before you know it."

It's fine, Micah told himself as he started up the steps.

Who cares what she thinks? She probably will make it back in time for her stupid aquarobics. Grandpa Ephraim will be better by then.

"Oh, it's nice of you to worry," said Aunt Gertrudis, "but I'm all right. Not that it's been easy with my brother and the boy. I do my best, but the situation just isn't healthy for either of them if you ask me. Honestly, I'm relieved that it's almost at an end."

Micah froze. His hand clutched the banister so tightly that all of the blood was pressed from his knuckles. *It's fine. It's nothing. You promised Grandpa Ephraim you would try to get along with her.*

He took a deep breath and let go of the banister.

"It's better this way really. It's even better for the boy in the long run. He doesn't need . . ."

Micah would never know what his aunt thought he didn't need, because he was somehow in the living room, and he was somehow yanking the phone line out of the wall, and he was somehow standing in front of Aunt Gertrudis, gasping like he'd run a race.

For just a moment, she was speechless, staring at him.

It was long enough for Micah to say exactly what he meant. "Something is *wrong* with you." He launched the words at her like missiles. "Why are you even here? You don't like me. You don't like Grandpa Ephraim. And even if Grandpa Ephraim loves you, I don't! I never will. Because you're *mean*."

It felt good to say it. And it felt dangerous, too. Aunt

Gertrudis stood up from the sofa, her lips quivering with rage.

"How dare you!" Her voice was a knife, but Micah was so angry that it couldn't cut very deep. "I take weeks out of my life. I come here to help my demented brother and you, you ungrateful little boy, and this is how you behave? Like some kind of barbarian! I should leave you here to rot!"

"Why don't you?!" Micah shouted. "I don't need you. Grandpa Ephraim doesn't need you. The Lightbender—"

Aunt Gertrudis laughed. It wasn't a happy laugh at all. "Is he going to wave his magic wand and save the day?" she said cruelly. "Is he going to fix what doctors and hospitals and expensive medicine can't?"

Micah's heart clenched, but he refused to back down. Backing down would mean letting her win, and in that moment, it felt like letting her win would be the worst thing that could happen to him. "You don't know anything."

"Oh, don't I?" Aunt Gertrudis spat. "This absurd fantasy is Ephraim's doing. I know how he is. And it's not *good* for you. It's *dangerous*. I'll put a stop to it right here and now. I guarantee you that!"

That was how The Fight started, and it went on for quite some time after that. It ended when Micah, shaking so hard he thought he might fly apart, screamed, "I hate you!" and Aunt Gertrudis replied, "Get out."

She pointed toward the door. "I'm not letting you near Ephraim until you've come to your senses and apologized."

Perhaps she meant for Micah to get out of the living

room, and not out of the house entirely. But she didn't object when he dragged an old sleeping bag out of the hall closet. She followed him upstairs and watched him stuff his backpack full of clothes and shoes. She watched him walk out the back door, which she locked behind him, and she watched through the window as he marched toward his tree house. When Micah looked back at her, she closed the curtains.

He guessed that was so she wouldn't have to watch him anymore.

The tree house smelled like new wood. It was missing one wall and the roof, but it was sturdy and well built. Micah's hands were still shaking with fury, but he managed to climb the rope ladder. He threw down his things and stared toward Grandpa Ephraim's window. It wasn't open. Micah hadn't thought that it would be, but he had hoped.

His grandfather liked to smell the fresh air when the weather was nice. Eventually, Aunt Gertrudis would wake Grandpa Ephraim up to give him his medicine, and he would tell her to open the window because he hated it when he couldn't see out.

She should have known that. Micah did.

But she doesn't even try to understand, he thought. If his aunt was trying to understand Grandpa Ephraim like Micah did, then a hundred things would be different. The window would be open. The coffee table in the

living room would still be covered in Old Maid cards, and
the refrigerator would still be full of orange soda. Most
importantly, Micah wouldn't be all alone in a tree house
while his grandfather was all alone in his room.

I hate you. He could still taste the words in his mouth,
and they tasted like the truth.

He wasn't a bother to Grandpa Ephraim, and Grandpa
Ephraim had never filled his head with nonsense. They
needed each other. If Aunt Gertrudis refused to see that,
then what else might she refuse to see? The Lightbender
could show up any minute, and she would think he was
the mailman. Or a burglar!

Micah set his jaw. He wouldn't let Aunt Gertrudis get in
the way. Not this time. He pulled a spiral-bound notebook
and a thick black marker out of his bag and sat facing the
window. The bottommost limb of the oak tree stretched
out toward the house. It wasn't close enough for Micah to
climb onto the windowsill, but he thought that it would
be close enough for him to have a conversation with his
grandfather when the window opened.

"The Plan" he wrote in large letters across the top of the
first page. Then he wrote, "Step One." This was as far as he
got before he had to stop and think.

Half an hour later, Micah had almost chewed the end
off of the marker, but he was no closer to an answer. He
slapped the notebook shut and threw the marker to the
floor. He watched it roll toward the edge of the platform.
He couldn't muster up the desire to stop it. It slowed down

until it almost wasn't moving, teetered on the edge for a moment, then fell.

"Ouch!"

Micah jumped at the sound of the voice below him. He crawled to the edge and peered over.

Jenny Mendoza was standing at the foot of the oak, rubbing one of her cheeks. It had a short black stripe on it where the marker had hit her, and she was smearing the ink toward her nose. "Yuck," she said. "Why did you throw a marker at me?"

"I didn't know you were there!"

She was still wearing the pink skirt she'd worn to school that day. It perfectly matched the pink bicycle helmet on her head. An adult-sized bike with a strange sort of wagon hooked to the back was parked beside her.

"What are you doing here?"

Jenny unhooked her helmet and clipped the straps around the bike's handlebars. "That woman in your house told me to go away. She was very grouchy."

"That's my aunt. Well, my great-aunt," said Micah. He thought "grouchy" was a remarkably mild description. "She said the same thing to me."

Jenny stretched her neck back so that she could see him. "I already called my parents at work, and I told them that Florence Greeber had invited me over to spend the night."

"She lives four houses down."

Jenny shuffled her feet. "She didn't really invite me. She doesn't even like me. I'm here to see you."

When he didn't reply, she added, "I'll be in trouble if I can't stay here. They'll know I lied." She pointed toward the wagon thing, and Micah saw through its clear plastic roof that it was full of books and craft supplies. "I've got everything we need to finish our project."

Micah didn't quite know what to think. After his conversation with Jenny in the craft closet, he hadn't been expecting something like this. Jenny didn't seem like the kind of girl who lied to her parents often. But he wasn't exactly in the mood for company.

"I'm kind of busy right now, Jenny."

She nodded. "I brought stuff for your grandfather. I found a book on traveling circuses at school, and I printed some things off the computer. I brought peanut butter crackers and tuna sandwiches, too."

Micah was impressed. All he'd managed to do this afternoon was get kicked out of the house and scribble a few bad ideas in his notebook. Jenny had showed up with a decent plan, a small library, and supper.

Even though he had messed up their project. Even though they had argued.

Jenny might not have much imagination, Micah realized, but she had a whole lot of something that was even more important. He pushed the rope ladder over the edge so that it unrolled toward the ground.

"You can come up," he said. "There's plenty of room."

As the sun set, the air grew cooler. Jenny put one of Micah's spare T-shirts on over her own clothes, since neither of them had a jacket, and they unfolded the sleeping bag to keep their legs warm. Micah was glad he had remembered to pack a flashlight and batteries for when it got dark. He was also glad that Jenny had come. Somehow, spending the night in the tree house didn't feel as much like a punishment when he had company.

"This isn't working," she said in a frustrated voice. "I'm following the instructions, but it looks all wrong."

She was hunched over the thing that was supposed to be their new quipu. It looked more like a rainbow-colored bird's nest to Micah.

A piece of tuna fell out of his sandwich onto *The Big Book of Big Tops*, and he brushed it off. "I'm not having much luck either," he admitted.

Jenny squinted at her string. She had brought a book on knot tying from the library, and a pile of thread and yarn from her mother's sewing shop. She had decided to assign a different type of knot to all of the letters of the alphabet so that she could spell out the names of every student in their class. It was a good idea, but Micah was pretty sure she wasn't going to manage it unless she stayed up all night.

"Done!" she announced. She held up a loopy mess of a knot.

Micah winced. "Here. Let me try."

She handed him a fresh strand of brown embroidery floss, and after a brief glance at the picture of the knot she had chosen, he started to tie. This wasn't like what he had tried to do in class today. He wasn't trying to make a knot that reminded him of anyone in particular, and as long as he was careful not to think too hard about Grandpa Ephraim while he worked, it was almost relaxing.

"What letter is this one supposed to be?" he asked.

"It represents *G*," Jenny said. "I'm trying to spell 'Giles.' Don't you need to read the instructions?"

"Not really." Micah twisted the string this way and that, and then he looped it back on itself *just so*. He held it out for Jenny to inspect.

Her eyes widened. "How did you do that? It's better than the one in the picture! It *looks* kind of like a *G*."

Micah shrugged, but he couldn't help being a little pleased at the compliment. "I'm good at knots. Grandpa Ephraim is too. It's kind of our thing."

"Do you think you could show me how? If I make many more mistakes I'm going to run out of string."

Micah looked down at the knot. It was tiny and perfect, and even though he knew exactly how he'd done it, he was pretty sure it wouldn't work for Jenny. "It would probably be faster if I did this part."

"Okay." She sounded relieved as she reached for *The Big Book of Big Tops*. "We'll trade jobs. I'm good at research anyway."

Micah didn't argue. At least working on the quipu made him feel like he was doing something useful.

Jenny flopped onto her stomach and opened the book to

the table of contents. "Maybe we've been going about this the wrong way," she said. "How did your grandfather hear about the circus? Did it come to his town every year? That might give us a clue."

"One day it was just there," Micah said. He tied another knot, and Giles Darby's name started to take shape. "Next to the beach where he used to play when he was a boy."

10

A PERFECTLY ORDINARY TRANSACTION

To reach his beach, Ephraim usually walked straight through town, past some tired old hotels and rickety apartments. But as he followed the sound of pipes and drums over the final dune, he saw that town was a good deal farther away than it ought to have been, as though it had been conjured to a new location over the course of the morning. A misty green meadow now rested between the dunes and the run-down buildings.

Large round tents with pointed tops were scattered in a haphazard circle in the middle of the green. Tiny, triangular flags decorated their center posts. Each tent was a different color of satiny cloth, and each had a different pattern stitched into it. Ephraim saw silver stars on a sapphire background and golden suns on ebony and thick crimson lines striping chocolate brown. Horses with braided manes and tails were tied to stakes between the tents, and as he approached, he thought, for just a moment, that he saw a tremendous white tiger stalking around the perimeter of the circle.

But of course that's ridiculous, he told himself. *Nobody would let a tiger run free.*

When he arrived, a curving metal sign over the top of the ticket taker's stand informed him that he had discovered a circus.

CIRCUS
MIRANDUS
MAGNIFICENT SINCE 500 B.C.

⋆ MR. M. HEAD, MANAGER ⋆

He was still considering the date, and whether or not such a thing might be true, when the ticket taker cleared his throat.

The man looked unusual. He was round in the middle and thin everywhere else, and he was hairy all over except for on the top of his head. He wore a tailcoat and a golden monocle and thick-soled boots covered in mud and hay. "Comin' in, young fellow?" he asked. "Got your ticket?"

"No, sir," Ephraim said. He also didn't have money, and he doubted that his mother would give him any considering his ongoing campaign against attending school.

"Shame." The man took his monocle off his eye, rubbed it on his sleeve, then put it back on the other eye. "You're just the age we like around these parts."

Ephraim knew he shouldn't waste the ticket taker's time when he wasn't a paying customer, but the music was still telling his feet to come closer to the tents, and his heart agreed with his feet. "I could help you with something maybe?" he suggested. "In exchange for a ticket? I could brush the horses. I'm good at it."

In fact, Ephraim didn't know the first thing about horses, but before the war he had sometimes watched his father brushing his mother's hair at night. He reasoned that it couldn't be very different.

The ticket taker shook his head. "Sorry. I'm not authorized for barterin'."

Ephraim was about to say that he was exceptionally good at tying knots, which would have been true, when another boy around his age appeared out of the mist.

"Ticket?" asked the man.

The boy nodded and reached into the pocket of his overalls. Ephraim thought it was strange that he had never seen this boy around town before, and that he wasn't in school. He thought it was even stranger when the boy pulled a spool of yellow thread out of his pocket and handed it to the ticket taker.

The man switched his monocle from one eye to the other again and squinted at the thread. "Two-hour ticket." He untied the velvet rope that blocked off the entrance to the circus, and he bowed. "Have fun."

The boy dashed through.

"That wasn't a ticket!" Ephraim protested. "It was thread!"

The ticket taker rolled his eyes. "Shows what you know. I've been at this job since the very beginnin'." He pointed up at the sign over his head. "The very beginnin'. I know what a ticket looks like."

Ephraim was about to argue, but the passenger in his boot, the one that had swum in when he tried to walk across the ocean to Europe, nibbled at his ankle. Inspiration bit Ephraim. "I've got a fish," he said. "Will that work?"

He pulled off his soggy boot and passed it to the man, who took it as though it were a perfectly ordinary sort of transaction.

"Oho!" he said, plucking the silvery fish out neatly between his thumb and forefinger and watching it wriggle. "What have you been up to, to get one of these? Haven't seen a week-long pass in an age."

"A week?" Ephraim hardly dared believe it. A whole

week at the circus in exchange for an annoying piece of seafood?

"A week," the ticket taker confirmed as he removed the rope from the entrance. "Mr. Head's been looking everywhere for this."

He held the squirming fish out to the side, dropped the boot to the ground, and bowed—lower than he had for the other boy—as Ephraim stepped past him into Circus Mirandus.

Circus Mirandus was the sort of place that filled you up to the top of your head. Ephraim spent the whole of his first day dashing from one tent to the next, seeing bits and pieces of the shows and people and creatures inside each one.

He met several Strongmen and watched one of them lift a girl right over his head using only the tip of his pinkie. Ephraim tasted candies that fizzed and popped, and he drank a dark blue fruit juice that made him sing opera for half an hour. He fed hay to an elephant that could do long division and chunks of meat to a vulture that could tell the future by plucking its own feathers.

It told him he would one day have a little sister.

"Really?" He wasn't sure how he felt about this news on the whole, since girls were confusing.

"*Oui*," said the vulture. (He was French.) "She eez going to be vairy not nice I am seeing. A steenky egg."

Ephraim decided he would have to wait until he met her.

He came back the next day, and the next. Sometimes he even stayed through the night. Circus Mirandus was always open, and it was never empty. Children Ephraim didn't recognize were everywhere he looked, but there were no adults except for the performers. On the third day, Ephraim asked the ticket taker, whose name he'd learned was Geoffrey, if grown-ups weren't allowed inside.

The man scratched his chin. "I'm a grown-up aren't I?" he said. "Silly question."

"I mean regular adults. People who aren't working here."

"Oh, *those*," Geoffrey said, as though adults were a kind of nasty vegetable. "It's not that they're not allowed so much as that they're not invited. They spoil the mood, you see."

Ephraim thought his mother would add to the mood, rather than spoil it. But she would hardly let him spend all day every day at the circus, so telling her was out of the question.

One of the best things about Circus Mirandus was that you couldn't make the wrong decision about what to see or do. Ephraim usually let his feet carry him wherever the circus's music led them, or he followed the smells of horses or caramels or smoke. On that particular day, Ephraim ignored the music and the smells, and instead, he chased a darting swarm of creatures that were sometimes butterflies and sometimes fairies, depending on how you tilted your head. Their wings hummed a lazy tune while they wove in and out of the crowd, and Ephraim followed. He tried to tell himself that he wasn't all *that* interested in catching one.

Eventually they grew tired of the game and flitted out of sight, and Ephraim found himself standing before the glittering silver tent of the Amazing Amazonian Bird Woman for the second time that week. Her show had been his favorite so far, and he wasn't at all disappointed when the chattering crowd swept him into her tent.

He spotted her immediately. He stared up, up, up, and there she was, climbing her ladder. Ephraim's breath caught. She was even prettier than he remembered. She was small, and she didn't seem to be *too* much older than him. Her eyelashes were so thick that they looked almost like feathers, and every time she fluttered them Ephraim was certain she was looking right at him.

Her whole costume was made of long white feathers, and Ephraim had a powerful urge to touch one. They looked as though they had been spun from clouds.

The tent was one of the biggest in the circus, but the only thing in it other than the audience and the Bird Woman herself was a tall platform. She climbed slowly to the top and whistled. A hundred birds in every color of the rainbow swirled out of a skylight in the tent's roof. They darted around the Bird Woman, who smiled at them so sweetly that Ephraim felt like his insides were melting.

She stood on the very edge of the platform for a long

time, turning slowly so that everyone could admire her. Then, without the slightest warning, she jumped.

The audience gasped as a single body, even Ephraim, who had seen it once before. There were no lines to hold the Bird Woman, no nets to catch her. You were sure that she was going to crash into the earth.

But she didn't.

She came within inches of the ground, and then, at the last second, she swooped up and circled gracefully around the room with her birds, singing a song that didn't have any words. She soared right over Ephraim's head, close enough that he could have reached out to her if he wasn't afraid of breaking the beautiful scene above him.

When she passed by him a second time, he thought he heard his name in her song, and he shivered. He wasn't sure what being in love felt like, but he thought it might be a little like this.

Eventually, Ephraim had to leave the Bird Woman's tent. A lot of the performers stayed behind after their shows to talk with the audience, but after the finale, when she flew through the skylight and disappeared into the sky, the Bird Woman didn't come back. Ephraim wasn't the only one who waited hopefully for her return, but he stayed longer than any of the other children before giving up.

Slowly, inevitably, he made his way toward the only place in the circus that intrigued him more than the Bird Woman's. The mysterious black tent. It had caught his attention on the very first day, partly because it had a board across the entrance with the words NO ADMITTANCE painted on it, but also because something felt different about it.

The area around the black tent was quieter than the rest of the circus, and the atmosphere was always charged. It felt to Ephraim as though lightning might strike there at any moment. The tent was such a deep black that looking at it would have been like looking down a well, except for the golden suns that decorated every inch of it. They glittered like polished coins on even the foggiest of days. As if the tent wasn't fascinating enough on its own, a Strongman, wearing a bowler hat, stood outside of it turning children away.

"The Man Who Bends Light is practicing a new routine," the Strongman had said in a clipped British accent when Ephraim asked why he wasn't allowed inside. "Interruptions could be lethal."

After hearing that, Ephraim couldn't resist walking past the tent every chance he got just in case it had reopened. But the board was always in place, and the Strongman was always watching.

When he reached the black tent that afternoon, Ephraim fully expected to be sent on his way as he usually was, but something had changed. Several children were waiting patiently behind a golden rope to be let in. Instead of a NO ADMITTANCE sign, a large poster had been fastened to the side of the tent.

·THE·
Man Who Bends Light

SON OF THE SUN
MASTER OF ILLUSIONS

·SHOWINGS TODAY AT·
NOON
TWO
AND MIDNIGHT

It was nearly two o'clock. Ephraim stepped into line behind a tall boy who wore no shirt despite how chilly the breeze was that day. The boy's broad shoulders were sunburned. Ephraim often noticed children wearing strange clothes or speaking with unfamiliar accents at the circus. He suspected that they must all have come to Circus Mirandus from different places, though he hadn't quite figured out how. He stared at the boy's shoulders until a gasp from the front of the line drew his attention.

The rope was vanishing.

It wasn't being taken away by one of the performers. It wasn't falling. It was simply ceasing to exist, as though it were dissolving into the air, particle by particle, until it was gone. The girl in the front of the line stared at the place where it had been with a puzzled look on her face.

"I reckon that means we're supposed to go in," said the boy with no shirt.

The girl took a tentative step.

"Awww . . . don't be chicken," said the boy.

She turned around to stick her tongue out at him, and then she straightened her skirt and stalked into the tent with her chin turned up.

The children around Ephraim jostled him as the line moved forward. The crowd seemed larger than it had before, and he worried that they might not all fit. But somehow, the inside of the black tent was much more spacious than its outside.

It swallowed them whole.

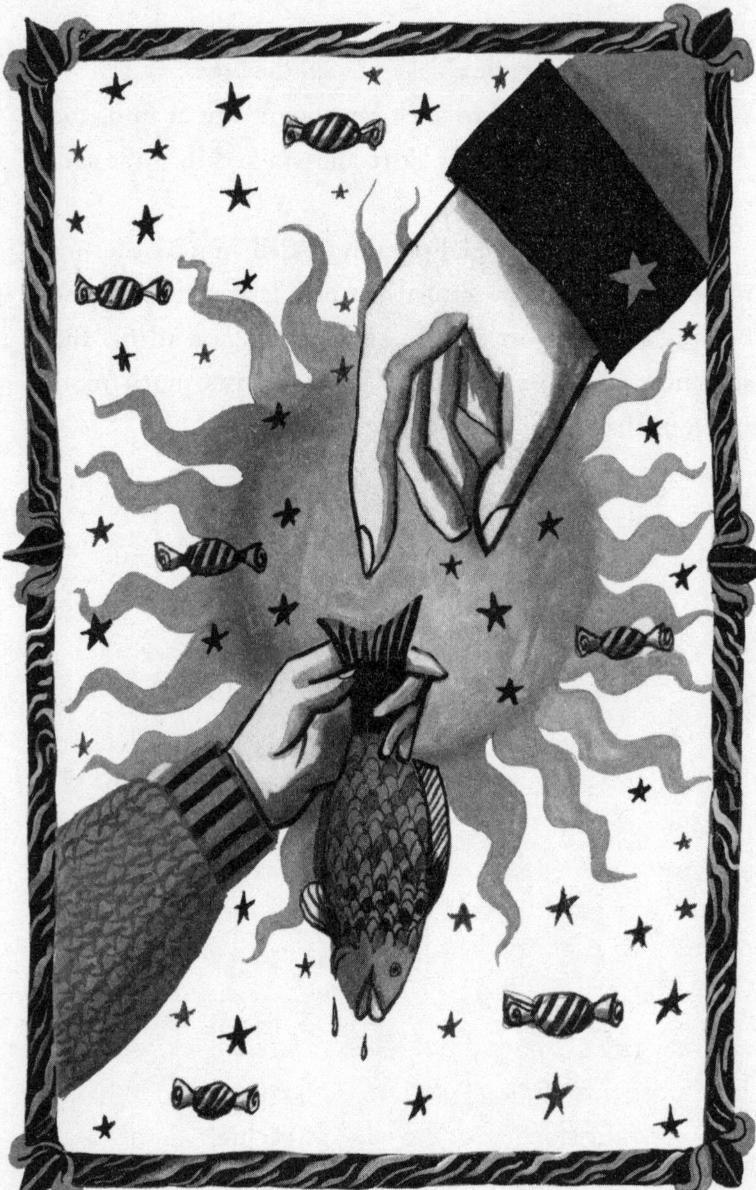

11

NORMAL BIRD BEHAVIOR

Many years later and under very different circumstances, another individual had the feeling that she had been swallowed whole, and not by anything as lovely as a circus tent. Chintzy had not enjoyed her time as a tourist in the Peal municipal sewer system. In fact, she was in an appallingly bad temper.

Chintzy was unusually large for her species to start with, and though she wouldn't admit it even to herself, she enjoyed a nice lemon cookie more often than was good for her. She couldn't find a big enough exit. After hours of flying through foul-smelling pipes and screeching even fouler words at the local rats, who wouldn't give her directions, she finally managed to squeeze herself out of the storm drain just down the street from the Tuttle house.

She looked like a week-old buzzard chick, and she smelled like a week-dead old buzzard. But Chintzy, as she was so fond of reminding the Man Who Bends Light, was a professional. She found a birdbath to dunk herself in to remedy the worst of the stench, and after she had collected herself, she headed straight for Ephraim Tuttle's bedroom window.

Of course, she didn't know it was being watched.

"It looks great," said Jenny. She was holding the flashlight like a spotlight over their finished quipu, and Micah could just make out her broad smile in the darkness.

They had stapled the whole thing to a poster board so that it wouldn't get tangled. It wasn't as fancy as Florence Greeber's pyramid, but Jenny was sure that they would get extra credit for making up their own version of a knot language.

Micah was just glad that she wouldn't fail the assignment because of him. His fingers ached, and tucked in his pocket, he had a small bundle of knots that had refused to become letters of the alphabet. All of these were the same, and all of them were like the Grandpa Ephraim knots from that morning. They were heavy in his pocket, but he wouldn't take them out. He didn't want Jenny to ask about them. They were private.

"I feel bad, though," she was saying. "I haven't found

anything about your grandfather's circus. I don't know where else to look, and I don't know how long—"

"It was nice of you to try," Micah interrupted. Whatever came after "how long," he didn't want to hear it. He didn't want to think about the fact that the letter had been sent two days ago, and the Lightbender had yet to appear. "I guess magical circuses don't make it into library books."

"We could call another circus on the phone." Jenny's voice was thoughtful. "They might know something."

Over the last few hours, the two of them had fallen into a pattern. Jenny pretended not to hear Micah when he said anything about Circus Mirandus that sounded impossible. And he pretended not to hear her when she talked about "the circus your grandfather based his stories on."

Micah enjoyed this arrangement. Jenny Mendoza was turning out to be an excellent friend.

"Would you like to go over the presentation one more time?" she asked.

Before he could say anything, there was a flapping sound overhead.

"Blasted humans," said a voice. "Can't be bothered to leave a window open for the messenger. Of course not. I have to do everything myself."

"What?" Jenny asked. "Micah, was that you?"

Micah knew who it was at once. "The flashlight!" he said. "Jenny, point it at the window."

Jenny spun toward Grandpa Ephraim's bedroom window. "Holy smokes!"

A filthy, mangy-looking bird was fluttering in front of the window. When the light touched her, she shrieked, "I've been spotted by the natives!"

"It *is* you!" Micah cried. He felt like cheering.

"Evasive maneuvers. Normal bird behavior is a go! Polly wants a cracker." The parrot smacked the glass with her beak. "Pretty birdy. Want a cracker. Open the window, you old goat, there are strange people in your tree watching me make a goose of myself."

"I'm not people," said Micah. "I'm his grandson."

He hurried to the edge of the tree house's platform and jumped to where he thought the big lower limb was without even stopping to check. The soles of his sneakers slipped sideways against the rough bark, but he managed to catch himself on his hands and knees before he could fall. "Please wait! I need to talk to you."

He started crawling across the branch toward the ugly bird.

"Don't," Jenny called. "I think something's wrong with it."

"Chimney!" said the parrot.

"Wait!" said Micah.

But it was no use. The parrot shot toward the roof of the house and out of sight.

Micah stood up on the limb, holding his arms out to either side of him for balance. "Come back!" he shouted. "The Lightbender! Is he coming soon?"

There was no reply.

Micah looked back to the tree house, and the glare of the flashlight in his face blinded him. He shielded his eyes with one hand. "You saw that didn't you?" he demanded. "You saw the magic parrot?"

Jenny lowered the flashlight so that he could see again. "I saw a parrot," she said slowly.

"That was *her*. The Lightbender's messenger."

Micah's knees were Jell-O. The messenger had come. They hadn't forgotten Grandpa Ephraim.

"Lots of parrots can talk," said Jenny, "but it did seem unusual. Did it say it was going to the chimney?"

Micah's shoes started to slip again, and he got back down on his hands and knees. "Yes," he said. "She's heading for my grandpa's room. I need to get back inside and talk to her before she gets away again."

"Didn't your aunt lock the door?"

He grimaced.

"Come off that branch," said Jenny. "You'll hurt yourself."

Micah started back toward the tree house. It was much slower, and more frightening, crossing the limb in the dark now that he was paying attention. Jenny grabbed him by the front of the shirt when he reached the platform and helped him pull himself up.

"I don't think you have to go back into the house."

Micah was already reaching for the rope ladder. "I'm not letting it escape before I find out everything I can about Grandpa Ephraim's miracle."

"No," said Jenny. "I mean I don't think it will be able to get back up the chimney. Most birds can't fly up a tight space like that, and that was a big bird. It's going to be trapped in the house unless someone lets it out."

"How do you know that?"

"My dad's a vet," she said. "Or . . . well, he will be. He's gone back to school for it."

"Oh." Micah pulled his hand back from the ladder. "It's a magical bird, though." He didn't have much experience with this sort of thing, but it seemed to him that a magical parrot shouldn't be stumped by something as simple as a chimney.

"It couldn't get through the window," Jenny pointed out. "So unless your grandfather gets up to let it out, it will still be there in the morning."

"I don't think he's well enough to get out of bed," said Micah. "Or the window would already be open."

They both sat, their legs dangling over the edge, and stared toward the window. After several long minutes, a light came on. It was hard to tell because of the curtains, but Micah thought it was Grandpa Ephraim's bedside lamp.

"It's in there," Jenny whispered.

"She's talking to him," said Micah. He shivered and wrapped his arms around himself. "I wish I could hear what they're saying."

Jenny patted him on the shoulder. "We can watch in

shifts. Just in case your grandfather *does* open the window for it. That way we won't miss anything."

"I'll go first," said Micah. "You should try to sleep."

He held his hand out for the flashlight, and she passed it to him. She crawled over to the sleeping bag and pulled it all the way up to her chin. She was so quiet after a little while that he thought she had fallen asleep, but then she said, "Micah?"

He pointed the light at her.

She blinked sleepily. "I'm glad Mrs. Stark made us partners."

Something warm uncurled in Micah's chest. "Me too, Jenny."

12

A SERIOUS
FAILING OF CHARACTER

Micah decided not to wake Jenny up for her turn on watch. He was so worried about Grandpa Ephraim, so curious about what might be happening behind the closed curtains, that he was sure he couldn't possibly be sleepy.

He kept the flashlight shining toward the house and ignored his yawns. A couple of moths, attracted to the beam of light, fluttered around his hands. He gave up shooing them after a short while, and watched their huge shadows flap against the house's pale siding.

A few feet away, his grandfather was talking to the Lightbender's messenger. Micah almost couldn't stand it.

He was missing what might be the most important conversation of his entire life.

To distract himself, he pulled the wad of knots that felt like his grandfather out of his pocket and examined them. They were so different from anything he'd made before. How could a knot feel like a person?

He rubbed one of them between his palms. It was warm and fraying, just like the others. And it was a little sad. He curled his fingers around it. It wasn't right. Grandpa Ephraim was sad now, maybe, but he hadn't been before.

Micah swung his feet back and forth so that the edge of the tree house's platform bit into the backs of his legs. When they'd been working together to build the tree house, he and Grandpa Ephraim hadn't been able to stop laughing and telling jokes. Now . . .

It just wasn't right.

He watched the shadows of the moths until his eyes began to feel heavy. His fingers were moving over the knot almost without his permission. They were tweaking here and tugging there. They were remembering sunny days and the smell of freshly sawn boards.

Micah only meant to close his eyes for a moment. He was trying to remember better. But one moment turned into several, and the new knot slipped out of his hands.

Jenny screamed.

Micah's eyes snapped open, and he scrambled to his

feet, suddenly wide awake. The flashlight had rolled away from him to rest against one of the tree house's walls, and it was pointing away from Jenny. She was a bulky, flailing shape on the floor.

"What's wrong?"

"Get it off! Get it off!" she shrieked.

"Let go of me!" squawked another voice. "Don't you *dare* grab my tail."

Micah headed for the light, but he tripped on his backpack in the dark. He landed flat on his stomach, missing the edge of the platform by inches.

"It *stinks*," Jenny wailed, just as Micah's fingers closed around the flashlight's handle and he whipped around.

The sight before him was bizarre. Jenny and the sleeping bag looked as if they'd had a fight to the death, and the bag had almost won. Its stuffing was oozing out of one corner, but it had managed to eat half of Jenny before it died. She seemed to be missing an arm and a leg, and the bag's zipper had gotten caught in her braids.

Jenny wasn't the sleeping bag's only victim. The Lightbender's parrot was lying on her back at the foot of the bag with her long claws caught in the stitching. She was ripping at the fabric with her beak.

Micah crawled forward. "The Lightbender's coming, right?" he asked the parrot. "He's going to help?"

He reached out to help free her feet, but she hissed at him.

"Micah?" Jenny's voice trembled. "It's just the bird isn't it? I . . . I can't see anything."

Micah stared at his new friend and realized with a guilty squirm that he probably should have helped her before interrogating the bird. Jenny's hair had been dragged over her face by the zipper's teeth, and she had to bend her neck sideways to keep it from pulling.

"It's okay, Jenny," he said. "You're just tangled up. I can fix it."

He helped her tug her arm and leg free first, and then he went to work on her hair. "What's that smell?" she asked after a few seconds.

Micah, who had almost managed to liberate Jenny's left braid, paused to sniff. Something did smell awful, like a toilet that hadn't been flushed in much too long. He looked around for the source of the odor, and his eyes landed on the parrot. He'd thought she was ugly at first, but now he could see that she was just extremely dirty. Patches of gleaming red feathers showed through the muck.

"I think the smell is the Lightbender's parrot."

The parrot turned her head toward Micah, and her pupils narrowed into pinpricks. "I'm my *own* bird, thank you very much."

"It smells like sewage," said Jenny. "I was asleep, and it *attacked* me."

Micah managed to unsnarl the last bit of her hair from the zipper, and they both stared at the bird. The flashlight was pointing right at her, and her feet were still caught in the sleeping bag.

"Selfish children these days," she muttered around

a beakful of cottony stuffing. "Won't even share a few delicious tidbits with the messenger. I blame television."

Micah realized then that the floor of the tree house was covered in peanut butter cracker crumbs.

"You ate our breakfast," Jenny accused. She turned to Micah. "I must have spread the sleeping bag out on top of some of our supplies last night. The bird wanted our food. I don't know how it got out of your house. The window's still shut."

"A trick I learned in Iceland, and don't call me *the bird*," squawked the parrot. "Like I'm some common chicken. It's 'Ms. Chintzy' to you two, or 'ma'am.'"

Micah leaned over Chintzy, just out of reach of her sharp beak. "Do you want some help?" he asked. "Ma'am? I could untangle your claws."

"I can do it myself. I'm a professional."

Micah nodded. He thought that Chintzy looked anything but professional, lying on her back with her feet stuck to a sleeping bag, but he couldn't risk offending her. He watched the parrot struggle.

"I need to talk to you about the Lightbender, ma'am," he said when he couldn't stand waiting any longer. "Is he coming? Will he be able to help my grandfather?"

"Oh, so you're Micah?" Chintzy shook a wad of stuffing out of her beak and looked at him. "You're not making the best first impression. Your friend *swatted* me, you know."

"You were *stealing*," said Jenny. She put her hands on

her hips, which looked a little silly, since she was still sitting on the floor.

"It's traditional to offer travelers a snack!"

"We were asleep. We didn't *offer* you anything."

"Well. A serious failing of character if you ask me," Chintzy squawked. "You're probably the kind of girl who doesn't leave cookies for Santa."

Both Jenny and Chintzy looked like they were puffing themselves up for a good long argument. Micah glared at them. "Stop it!" he said. "Who cares about the crackers? What about Grandpa Ephraim?"

"Sorry," Jenny said. "I forgot."

Chintzy didn't apologize, but at least she didn't seem inclined to continue the fight. Instead, she tilted her beak toward him. "Your grandfather doesn't want the sort of thing people usually ask for, you know."

Micah leaned closer to Chintzy. She eyed his hands warily, and he shoved them under his armpits to prove that he didn't mean to grab her without her permission. "I don't think it's that strange," he said eagerly. "We need the Lightbender to save him. He can do that, right? Is he coming?"

Chintzy blinked her wrinkled gray eyelids a few times. She bent her neck to her chest and plucked one of her own feathers almost absentmindedly. Micah wasn't sure, but he thought it was a nervous gesture.

He took a deep breath. "He *is* coming? Soon?"

"Of course," said Chintzy at once. "He promised your

grandfather, so he's coming. We're all coming. Looking forward to the change in climate myself."

A small firework burst in Micah's chest. The Lightbender was coming. "And he'll be able to help Grandpa Ephraim, won't he?"

He didn't wait for an answer. Instead, he turned to Jenny. "He can do the most amazing things," he told her excitedly. "You wouldn't believe my grandpa's stories. I haven't told you everything yet, but just wait. You'll see."

"Umm," said Jenny.

"Well," said Chintzy. She sounded uncomfortable, but Micah thought that anyone with her toenails caught in a sleeping bag had good enough reason.

"What?" he asked.

"I'm just the messenger." Chintzy plucked another chest feather. "Not the authority on how these things are done. And I don't think I should talk about it with you before I've done my messengerly duties. Seeing as you're neither sender nor recipient."

Jenny narrowed her eyes. "That sounds like an excuse."

"It's okay," Micah said quickly. "Can I do anything to help? When the Lightbender comes, I mean." He would keep Aunt Gertrudis out of the way. He wasn't sure how, but he would do it. She couldn't be allowed to interfere with Grandpa Ephraim's miracle.

"You'll need to do a lot," said Chintzy. "Get to Circus Mirandus for one thing."

"I thought it was coming here," Jenny said before

Micah could get the exact same words out of his mouth.

"It will," Chintzy replied. "But, well, I'm not sure how the Head will want to deal with . . ." She clicked her beak a few times. "Just keep a sharp eye out."

"I can do that." Micah wasn't completely sure what Chintzy meant, but if he had to do it for Grandpa Ephraim, he would. And having the chance to see Circus Mirandus himself! He hadn't dared to hope for it.

"That's good. Excellent. The Man Who Bends Light, the Head—well, I can't imagine what they'll say about all of this," Chintzy babbled half to herself. "This isn't the sort of thing we usually deal with."

"I'm not sure I understand," Micah said. "Grandpa Ephraim's miracle . . ."

Chintzy threw one wing out dramatically. "No more questions! I'll do my job and you'll do your job, and everything will work out for the best if it works out for the best."

Micah nodded, even though a thousand questions had started fighting to get out of his mouth as soon as she said "no more."

Chintzy jabbed the sleeping bag with her beak a few more times and then hissed at the stitching. She turned back to Micah. "The first part of your job," she said, "is helping me with *my* job."

For a moment, Micah wasn't sure what she meant. She didn't let him wonder for long.

"Get this human torture device off me!" she shrieked.

"Oh! Sure." He pulled his hands out from under his armpits and reached for her scaly feet. "It will only take a second. I'm really good at things like this."

"So I've heard," the parrot muttered. She eyed him suspiciously while he tugged at the stitches that had trapped her claws. "If you ever tell anyone about this," she said, "you're going to lose a thumb."

"That's not very nice," said Jenny.

"And an earlobe," Chintzy added.

Micah and Jenny stayed up talking for a long time after Chintzy vanished into the night sky. They couldn't quite agree on what their conversation with the parrot had meant.

"It was hiding something," Jenny said for the third time. "It dodged a lot of your questions."

Micah shook his head. "I don't think *she* would do that. Anyway, they're coming soon. Maybe even tomorrow. I'll know for sure what's going on then."

Jenny shook her head. "If it's really flying back to Bolivia to deliver a message it will take days and days. And moving a whole circus! That will take ages."

"They have ways." Micah didn't know what these ways might be, but he was confident. "Chintzy is a *magical* parrot. It's a *magical* circus."

Jenny didn't reply.

"You can't argue with that!" Micah exclaimed. "She talked just like a human, only with more squawking and threatening."

Jenny sighed. "It *was* a very peculiar parrot. I've never heard of one that smart."

Micah beamed.

"But it's probably been genetically modified!" she said. "Of course. Scientists can do that, I think. That explains it."

Cracker crumbs crunched under Micah as he flopped down onto his back and groaned. "You have an answer for everything."

When Jenny didn't say anything, he rolled over onto his side to look at her. She was staring down at the flashlight in her lap, flicking the switch back and forth.

"What's wrong?" Micah couldn't think of what he might have said to upset her.

"Nothing," Jenny said quickly. She didn't take her eyes off the flashlight. "It's just. . . It's good to have answers, isn't it?" She bit her lower lip. "I *like* knowing things. Only it bothers some people."

Micah remembered the girls in class that morning, laughing at Jenny behind her back. "It doesn't bother me."

"Okay," said Jenny.

"Really. I think it's good that you're so smart," he said. "And if you think Chintzy might be a science experiment, it doesn't matter."

She finally turned to him.

"You're helping me," Micah said. "You're my friend. That's what matters."

A Change
in the Wind

"**F**EATHERS! Why is your room covered in *feathers*?!"

Micah's eyes snapped open, and he scrambled to his feet. The tree house was bright with early morning sunshine. "What was that?" he asked.

"*Who* was that?" said Jenny.

Then Micah realized that Grandpa Ephraim's window was open. Aunt Gertrudis appeared a moment later. She held a dustpan full of dingy red feathers at arm's length, as if they were contagious, and tipped them outside. She spied Micah in the tree.

"You," she said. "I don't know how you did this, but I'll

find out. I'll deal with you after school." She slammed the window.

Jenny stared at Micah with eyes as round as quarters. "Your aunt can't be serious, can she? You weren't even there."

Micah shrugged.

"But that's not fair!" she protested.

"It's fine," said Micah. "She'll be gone as soon as Grandpa Ephraim gets well."

"If you say so." Jenny peered through the branches of the oak. The sky was pale blue and cloudless, and the sun peeked over the rooftops across the street. "What time do you think it is?"

Of course there wasn't a clock in the tree house, but Micah spotted something just as good. "Five minutes before the bus comes."

Jenny blinked. "You have a watch?"

He pointed across the street. A mop of familiar bright red curls was visible between two houses for a moment before a neighbor's privacy hedge hid it from view.

"Was that Florence?" Jenny asked. "That wasn't Florence was it?"

Micah nodded. "She always shows up five minutes before the bus comes."

Jenny made an odd squeaking sound and flung herself at the rope ladder. "We have a presentation today!" she shouted as her feet hit the ground. "I can't get dressed for a presentation in five minutes!"

Micah wasn't sure why she needed to change clothes when she was wearing a mostly clean outfit from the day before, but he didn't have time to ask. She grabbed a bundle from the wagon attached to her bike and shot toward the house.

Micah suspected that if his aunt hadn't unlocked the door yet, Jenny Mendoza would burst right through it.

Micah scuffed his feet against the floor of the school bus. He tapped his fingers against his knees. He checked the quipu for any tangles, and when he didn't find any, he checked it again. He looked out of the finger-smudged windows. A lot.

Surely, the ride to school had never taken this long before. Surely, something important was about to happen. Any second, they'd turn a corner, and the Lightbender would be there, or Chintzy would appear, or Micah would hear the circus music over the grumble of the bus's engine.

But all he heard was Jenny, who was rehearsing their report under her breath, and Florence, who was making annoyed huffing noises and kicking the back of their seat.

"I think I'd better go home with you after school today," Jenny said suddenly. She looked up from her notes. "Your great-aunt sounded upset. I'll explain to her that we were in the tree house all night, so she won't be mad at you about the feathers."

Micah's feet stopped scuffing. *"No."* Aunt Gertrudis was not the kind of grown-up who appreciated explanations.

"Don't you want me to come over? I have to go back to get the bicycle anyway."

"You can come over, but you ought to avoid Aunt Gertrudis. I do." He stole another quick glance out the window. Nothing.

Jenny crossed her arms over her chest. "She shouldn't be allowed to throw you out of your own house. You need to tell someone."

"I like sleeping in the tree house."

"Seriously, Micah," she said. "Your grandfather would want to know."

He would. But, Micah didn't want to upset him, especially not when Circus Mirandus was about to arrive.

"Hmmmkay?" It was a good sound in his opinion. It might have meant yes, and it might have meant no, but it satisfied Jenny. She went back to her notes.

As the bus pulled into the elementary school's drive, Micah searched for something out of the ordinary. The leaves hung limp from the branches of the spindly trees in front of the school. A wisp of cloud sat frozen overhead. The teachers' parking lot was still. The view was the same as everywhere else. Circus-free.

Micah felt like he was smothering.

When he and Jenny reached the classroom, they saw that the order for presentations had been posted on the board.

"Oh. We're next to last," said Jenny. She sounded disappointed.

"At least we're not first," Micah replied.

She sighed.

"You *wanted* to go first?"

"Everyone will be tired of listening by the time we go! They won't pay any attention to us."

He would have thought that was a good thing. Much less pressure.

But Florence stepped into the room a moment later and grimaced when she saw her name at the very bottom of the board. She shot Jenny a ferocious look. As he headed for his desk, Micah decided that being very smart must also make you just a little bit crazy.

The presentations started right after the Pledge, with Nathan giving a failed indoor boomerang demonstration that Mrs. Stark didn't appreciate at all. Micah tried to focus, but he was fighting a losing battle. He mulled over his conversation with Chintzy, trying to figure out whether Jenny might have been right last night. *Had* the parrot been holding something back? Why would she?

He slouched in his desk and shoved his hands into the pockets of his jeans. The knots from last night were still there. He didn't pull them out. They were all the same sad Grandpa Ephraim knot, except for one.

The knot he'd been fiddling with when he'd fallen asleep had been transformed. It was no longer fraying at the edges. Instead, it was as tight as a clenched fist, and when Micah held it, he could almost hear someone whistling. He let his fingers brush against it now, and he took a shuddering breath.

This knot was his grandfather, too, but not the Grandpa Ephraim who was stuck in bed all day long. This was him at his best, whistling and telling jokes, swinging Micah around in dizzy circles and tying a perfect rope ladder. This was the Grandpa Ephraim that Micah missed every minute of every day, and only the Lightbender could bring him back.

He forced himself to let go of the new knot. If he kept rubbing it, it wouldn't be long before it was just a puff of fiber.

What if I miss something? Micah thought, not for the first time. Or, even worse—*what if I've already missed it?*

"And this is an example of an Incan quipu."

Jenny delivered their presentation in a clear, almost-not-nervous voice. Micah shifted his weight from foot to foot and tried not to look out of place standing beside her. "Micah created his own alphabet out of knots and made a strand for each of you."

It wasn't completely terrible, as far as presentations went, but Micah was glad that he didn't actually have to say anything except for, "Thank you for your attention."

A minute later, Jenny cleared her throat, and Micah realized that it was his turn. He lifted the quipu's poster board up over his head so that the kids in the back row could see it. "Thank you for your attention," he said.

The whole class, except for Florence, applauded. Micah propped the quipu against the wall beside a dreamcatcher, and he and Jenny returned to their separate desks.

Back in his seat, Micah finally saw the quipu he'd made from his classmates' perspective. It did look impressive, he guessed, especially if you didn't know much about knot tying. The multicolored knots made a bright, elaborate fan against the white background, and though Micah suspected that his classmates wouldn't be able to, he could read the quipu from here without even touching the knots. The little *G* knots really did look like *G*'s somehow, and the little *R* knots looked like *R*'s. He examined it for a while, trying to feel happy about it, but his eyes were inevitably pulled toward the classroom window.

Still no Lightbender, still no Chintzy, just half-opened blinds and sky.

Jenny caught his eye. "What's wrong?" she mouthed.

Micah shook his head. Disheartened, he stared down at his notebook. Florence and her partner were talking about how the ancient Egyptians would stick little spoons up people's noses and stir their brains into goo before they turned them into mummies. Micah had the feeling that this should have been riveting, but he couldn't quite make himself care enough to take notes.

Instead, he drew a picture of a spoon at the top of his sheet of paper. Maybe Chintzy had *forgotten* to tell him something important. She seemed very smart, but she was a bird after all.

He scribbled until the spoon was a dark gray blob. Maybe she hadn't explained to the Lightbender how urgent the problem was. Grandpa Ephraim had to have his miracle right now. Not in days and days. Or maybe—

Something brushed against Micah's ear.

He looked over his shoulder. All of his classmates seemed to be focused on the presentation or on their notebooks. Desks squeaked and creaked as they shifted in their seats. Nobody was paying attention to Micah. He went back to his spoon.

He would have to see Grandpa Ephraim this afternoon no matter what Aunt Gertrudis said. Chintzy might have explained more to him. They had talked for hours.

Micah's ear tickled again. Both of his ears tickled. Because . . . because his hair was moving in the—

His pencil lead snapped. *I'm inside,* he thought. *It's impossible.*

But Micah was sure that the feeling against the back of his neck, the thing stirring his hair around his ears, was a faint breeze. He took a shuddering breath and let it out. The breeze didn't stop. Slowly, as though he might scare it off, he turned in his desk.

All around him, pencils were scratching against paper and feet were tapping against chair legs. No one else had noticed. No one else felt it. But the pages of Micah's notebook were rustling in the tiny breeze now, and it *wasn't* his imagination.

Fresh air filled his lungs as he gasped. *This must be it. This is it! What do I do?*

His notebook rustled again, and he looked down.

The sketch of the spoon unraveled, every line Micah had scrawled coming apart from every other and flowing into a new shape before his eyes.

An arrow, pointing toward the front of the room.

Micah looked past Florence and her partner and their perfect pyramid to the thing that the arrow was pointing at. The wind wasn't just blowing through the classroom, he realized. It was doing something. And it was doing it to Micah's quipu.

The strands of the quipu shivered in the breeze. They braided themselves in and out of one another. They twirled and snaked until the strands didn't say Giles Darby or Micah Tuttle or Nathan Borgle, or any of the names of his other classmates. The breeze rearranged Micah's very own knots to write a message that only he would be able to read:

Midnight.
Follow the wind.

In the time it took for him to blink, the quipu went back to being a quipu, but it didn't matter. Micah had seen it.

His eyes locked on the window, where, at last, there was something worth looking at. Leaves and twigs and old gum wrappers zipped past, caught up in a gale of wind that might have come straight out of Grandpa Ephraim's story.

THE MAN WHO
BENDS LIGHT

The tent of the Man Who Bends Light was dim and warm when Ephraim entered. The only illumination came from a few colorful oil lanterns that burned near the roof. Stands for seating ringed the center of the room, where a polished black circular stage dominated the floor. Ephraim found a spot in one of the less crowded sections and waited for the show to begin.

As soon as the last members of the audience had taken their seats, the tent flap closed and all of the lanterns flickered out. Not a speck of light made it through the fabric of the tent for Ephraim to see by. He heard the boy who had waited in line in front of him swear, and a girl sitting nearby whimpered.

"I hate the dark," she said just loudly enough for Ephraim to hear. "I really do."

Ephraim wasn't afraid of the dark, but he wasn't a great fan of it, either. Fortunately, just a few moments after everything turned black, a pinprick of gold appeared in the center of the tent.

Everyone went quiet, and Ephraim was sure that, like him, they were all staring at the small ball of light with fascination. It grew slowly at first, but then it picked up speed. Within a minute, Ephraim was shielding his eyes from the miniature sun pulsing in the heart of the room. The light was so strong that it filtered through his eyelids and made him see tiny bursts of color.

Then, just when he thought that the radiance was too powerful to bear, it faded. He cautiously squinted through one eye. The sun had turned into a rather spectacular pile of fruit.

The fruits were twice the size of Ephraim's fist, and they were a bright yellow that blushed red on one side. A galaxy of swirling golden pinpricks over the pile made it the brightest spot in the tent. Children whispered curiously to one another as, one by one, they opened their eyes.

"Have you ever tasted the flesh of the mango fruit?" A voice murmured in Ephraim's ear.

He whipped around, but nobody was sitting as close to him as the voice sounded.

"It tastes like the sun," the voice whispered in his other ear.

A man appeared next to the pile of mangoes. He was tall with shaggy blond hair, and he wore a battered brown leather coat that swished against the stage even though he was standing still. The man leaned backward into thin air and crossed one ankle over the other, as though he were resting against a solid wall.

He flicked his wrist. A mango leaped from the pile into one of his hands, and a sharp knife materialized in the other. The man slowly cut a wedge out of the fruit, which was the color of an egg yolk inside, and he bit into it. Juice dripped from his fingers.

A strange, sweet smell reached Ephraim's nose. He had never eaten any fruit more exotic than an orange, and he knew right down to the soles of his boots that the mangoes on the stage would be a hundred times more delicious than anything he had ever tasted. But approaching the man in the leather coat was the sort of idea that was a little too thrilling to be taken seriously.

The others seemed to have the same thought. Many of them were shifting in their seats, and Ephraim even heard a few people smacking their lips, but nobody stood up.

Just when it seemed that they might have to sit there all day, watching the man eat the mango with his gleaming knife, a dark-skinned boy sitting near the stage spoke up. "What's the sun taste like then?" he asked boldly.

The man's lips stretched into a smile. "Why don't you tell me?"

A single mango rolled across the stage toward the boy

who had spoken. He stared at it for a moment then bent to pick it up. It fell into neat slices in his hand. He brought one of them to his mouth and took a tiny bite.

His eyes widened.

The man laughed and flicked his hand again. The whole pile of mangoes toppled slowly and began to roll in every direction. Hands reached out from the audience to snatch them up as soon as they came within reach. When Ephraim caught one, it sliced itself for him, and juice ran down his knuckles.

Surprised, he accidentally dropped a couple of slices, and they evaporated before they could hit the ground. He stared at the remaining fruit in astonishment. Was it even real? It looked real and felt real and smelled real. He picked a particularly delicious-looking wedge and bit into it. It tasted mostly like the sun and just a little like his mother's famous peach pie. That was real enough for Ephraim.

The man strode to the center of the stage, and the gold sparks danced around him. "I am the Man Who Bends Light," he said. "Watch, and I will show you magic. Watch, and I will show you your dreams."

Ephraim's dreams had never been half as wonderful as the things he saw that day.

The tent faded out of existence, and Ephraim opened his eyes to a world made out of sparkling white and icy blue. He breathed sharp air into his lungs. A frosty wind stung his cheeks. Behind him, something made an odd trumpeting sound, and when Ephraim turned to see what it was, his booted feet crunched in the snow.

Ephraim wasn't alone in this strange new place. A line of stout black-and-white birds waddled past. They were the trumpeters. When he looked around he saw that there were other children nearby as well. The Lightbender, as Ephraim had decided to call him for convenience's sake, had somehow brought his whole audience to Antarctica to see penguins.

One after another, Ephraim's group of penguins fell on their bellies and slid across the ice. They were fat and sleek. Ephraim reached out toward the nearest one, and it snapped at him with its beak.

"Honk!"

"All right." He raised his hands into the air. "I won't pet you."

The penguin eyed him suspiciously then went back to skidding on its belly. Ephraim tagged along after it. He had only ever seen illustrations of penguins before, and he'd thought that they looked solemn, as though they had dressed for a funeral. But they were such funny birds in person. They paddled against the ice with their wings and feet just like they were swimming. They trumpeted and nipped at one another while they played a rowdy game of follow the leader right to the edge of the ice.

Ephraim stopped a few feet away from that edge. The ocean was a blue so deep it was almost black. He wasn't sure what kind of creatures swam in water that dark and cold, but he felt certain they had very sharp teeth. The penguins honked their good-byes and splashed in without a trace of fear. Ephraim waved as the last disappeared beneath the waves.

Before he could feel disappointed that they had gone, the world changed again.

A chariot pulled by four horses roared past. The air was made of dust and heat, horse sweat and sunlight. The children from the Lightbender's show had joined an enormous crowd of ancient Romans who were cheering for charioteers as they raced around a track at violent speeds. The girl beside Ephraim shrieked as another chariot charged by them.

"Are you okay?" he shouted over the noise of the crowd.

"I'm not sure!" she shouted back.

He understood. They were so close to the track that he could feel every hoofbeat. It was like thunder in his chest. And the charioteers! They drove their horses so wildly around the curves that Ephraim was sure they were going to crash. The chariots would splinter, and the drivers would be ground between hard earth and pounding hooves. It was almost too much, but at the same time, as the screams of the crowd swelled around him, Ephraim wished it would never end.

He opened his eyes as wide as he could, and he tried to take in every bit of it. *I am inside history,* he realized. *And it is so much more than it is in books.*

When the race ended, Ephraim found himself watching a meteor shower over a desert at night. Then he stood on the edge of a cliff, looking down at a sprawling city. He watched a fawn being born in a meadow. He tasted strange spiny fruits that were almost as good as mangoes. Sometimes he was with the others. Sometimes he was alone. For a long time, he stood at the prow of an old sailing ship by himself and watched a pod of whales. They breached the roiling surface of the sea and shot white geysers into the air.

Each new experience seemed better than the last, but when Ephraim found himself traveling on a log raft down a wide black river, he knew he must be in the best place of all—the jungle. The air smelled of damp soil and decaying vegetation, and the humidity plastered his hair to his forehead. Giant spiderwebs stretched from tree to tree overhead, and insects hummed in his ears.

Ephraim's father was a fan of adventure stories, and sometimes before bed, he would read to Ephraim about great explorers of the past. Father liked to learn about famous sailors, but Ephraim's favorite stories had always been about the deep jungles of the world. Pretty much all of the sea had been sailed, as far as he was concerned. The jungle was different. There were parts of the forests so hidden that no man had ever seen them. And that meant that a brave someone, maybe a brave someone named Ephraim Tuttle, could be the very first.

The raft drifted lazily toward the riverbank, and animals with bright eyes watched from the shadows as Ephraim made his way ashore. Mud sucked at his feet. Leaves as big as umbrellas slapped his face. *Real jungle mud,* he thought happily. *Real jungle leaves!*

He found a twisting path through the forest and followed it. When a rustle overhead caught his attention, he looked up to see monkeys swinging through the canopy. They moved through the trees so easily, like it was nothing special at all. *They could,* thought Ephraim, *be a whole new species of monkey. I could be the very first person to see them ever.*

This was such a wonderful idea that he decided it must be true.

He walked on, trying to see everything at once and failing miserably. The jungle was the most alive place he had ever been. Centipedes as long as his arm scurried along the ground. The monkeys chattered overhead. Butterflies the size of swallows drank from jewel-colored flowers in the dappled light.

It's almost perfect, Ephraim thought.

He stopped walking. *Almost?* he asked himself. He was traveling through the heart of the jungle, just like a great explorer. *What could be more perfect than that?*

"My father," he said. The jungle flickered around him like it was trying to decide whether it ought to be something else. Suddenly, Ephraim felt a hand on his shoulder. The Lightbender towered over him, his face expressionless.

"Are you quite certain?" he asked. "It will not be real, you know."

Somehow, Ephraim knew what he was asking. He swallowed the lump in his throat. "I . . . I'm sure."

15

EPHRAIM'S CHOICE

The jungle dissolved into a blur of color, and Ephraim found himself at home. He was in his very own living room, standing in front of his very own mother. She had tears in her eyes, but she was smiling.

"It's over sweetheart," she said. "The war is over."

For a moment, Ephraim couldn't move his lips. He hadn't known what it would feel like to hear those words.

"And your father is coming home," she said.

It felt like taking a breath of air after being underwater for much too long.

"How?" Ephraim struggled to push the words out. "How did it end?"

She told him how, and he thought, *Of course. Of course*

that is how it ended. That is the only good way for it to have ended.

The war had ended all at once and very calmly. It was as if, between one moment and the next, all the mothers of all the soldiers in the world had checked their clocks and realized that their children had been out playing for too long. The mothers set aside their laundry or their piecrusts or their welding torches, and they stepped out their front doors.

"Davey!" they called. "Klaus! Pierre! It's time to wash up for supper."

The soldiers shook hands with one another and wished one another well. Then they raced back to their mothers, or to their wives and sons.

"Your father is on his way," said Ephraim's mother. "He'll be here any min—"

Obadiah Tuttle stepped into the living room before Ephraim's mother could finish her sentence. He was wearing his uniform, and his chest was decorated with medals and ribbons. "Oh, Obadiah!" Ephraim's mother swayed as though she might faint.

Corporal Tuttle grabbed her around the waist, and then he kissed her. Right on the mouth.

Ephraim thought the whole thing was satisfyingly heroic. A moment later he was swept up into a hug so strong it might have cracked his ribs if his heart hadn't already been pressing against them from the inside. He smelled his father's favorite licorice candy. He felt the scratch of whiskers against his cheek.

"I was so scared you wouldn't come back," he said. He had never said it aloud before, but it was safe to say it now.

"I had to go. I'm sorry. I had to."

Ephraim touched one of the medals on his father's chest. "You were very brave," he said. "I bet you helped lots of people."

"Lots," his father said warmly. "But none of them were you."

Ephraim wiped his damp eyes against his father's uniform. "I wrote you letters. I wrote you so many."

His father kissed the top of his head. "I know," he whispered. "I followed them home."

Ephraim attended every show that the Lightbender had for the rest of the week. He even skipped the Amazing Amazonian Bird Woman's flying show so that he could make sure he was the first person in line. No matter how many times he experienced it, he never grew tired of the magic. The shows were all very close to the same, but never quite identical, so Ephraim could look forward to seeing the deep jungles of the world without having the same monkeys chatter at him in the same way that they had the last time he'd visited.

The only part that never changed was the end. Ephraim's father always came home.

More than any other thing he'd seen at Circus Mirandus, Ephraim carried the Lightbender's shows inside him. A world that had such magic in it must not be as awful as he had sometimes feared. Having experienced it, he thought he might be able to leave his beach behind and be brave while he waited for his father's real homecoming. Maybe, he could even go back to school.

What Ephraim wanted, more than anything else in his last days at Circus Mirandus, was simple but impossible. He wanted to walk up to the Lightbender after the show. He wanted to stick out his hand and say, "Thank you. My name is Ephraim Tuttle, and you have *changed* me."

He tried to do this every day, but at the end of each show he found himself horribly afflicted by nerves. The Lightbender had only spoken directly to Ephraim the one time, and in his more unreasonable moments he convinced himself that he had imagined the conversation. Telling another person that they have *changed* you for the better is no small matter, and Ephraim knew it.

But on the last day, the day his ticket expired, he also knew he had to succeed.

He worried himself into a state throughout that final show, so much of a state that he couldn't even remember seeing Antarctica. When everyone else filed out, he held on to his place in the stands with both hands and both knees so that he wouldn't run away.

The Lightbender watched the others go, and then he turned and noticed Ephraim, clinging to his seat like a stubborn barnacle. He smiled. "I think you can let the bench go," he said. "I have never yet seen it try to escape from a child. Did you enjoy the show today?"

It was really unfortunate timing on the Lightbender's part, because Ephraim had just worked himself up to say his piece, and being asked a question tossed him off balance. He stood up and threw his hand out in the general direction of his hero and said, "Ephraim Tuttle, very much, what's yours?"

The Lightbender tipped his head. "A pleasure to meet you again, Ephraim," he said. "I am the Man Who Bends Light. If I ever had another name, I have forgotten it."

Then he shook Ephraim's hand firmly.

Poor Ephraim, feeling twice as embarrassed as he had before, was silent. *If I can't say what I mean to,* he thought, *I'll have to say something else or he'll think I'm deranged.*

"I think you're just the most . . ." he said. "That is, you've no idea how much I . . . the things you showed me were so . . ."

Ephraim was sure that even his toes were blushing. *Say something,* he told himself. *Say anything.*

He looked down at his boots. "Would you like to see a magic trick?" he blurted.

He and the Lightbender both blinked at each other in surprise. Neither of them had thought *that* particular offer would be the result of their conversation.

"No one has ever asked me that before," the Lightbender said. He seemed to consider the question very seriously.

"Yes," he said at last. "Yes, I would like to see whatever you have to show me."

So the Lightbender sat down in the front of the stands, and Ephraim climbed up on the stage and performed the only magic trick he knew. He took the grubby lace out of one of his boots and set about tying a knot of great complexity. It had so many twists and turns that you couldn't follow it with your eye, and looking at it, you were certain that it could never be undone.

Ephraim held it out to the Lightbender and said, "Try to untie it."

The Lightbender poked it and tugged out strands and unraveled the bits that he could, but whatever he pulled at only made the knot look knottier. He smiled.

"I can't."

Then Ephraim reached out with a single finger and touched one strand, *just so*, and instead of a knot, there was a bootlace. He bowed low, and the Lightbender laughed.

"What a lovely bit of magic, Ephraim Tuttle. Thank you for showing me." He patted the seat next to him, and Ephraim took it.

Suddenly, talking wasn't so difficult after all. Ephraim asked questions about the circus, and he told the Lightbender about the war and his father and mother. He told him about writing letters every day and about his plans to become a train robber or maybe an archaeologist or maybe a jungle explorer.

"I worried when you said you wanted to see your father," the Lightbender confessed.

"Why?"

The Lightbender rubbed the side of his nose. "I am not always sure how far I should take my illusions. I don't want to do more harm than good."

Ephraim wasn't quite sure he understood. "Because I might have been sad when it was over?"

"Yes."

"I knew it wasn't real, though," said Ephraim. "Deep down I knew it was a show, so it was okay when it ended. It's not like you tricked me. That would have been different."

Something dark and pained crossed the man's face then, but it disappeared so quickly Ephraim thought he must have imagined it. "I am glad to know that," said the Lightbender. "Tell me more about your magic. It was rather astonishing, and I am not easily astonished."

Ephraim squinted at him. When he decided that he was not being teased, he grinned. "My father taught me. He can tie all sorts of knots. I can, too. The one I showed you is the best, though."

"I agree," said the Lightbender. "I have never seen a better knot."

Ephraim felt like he might float right off the bench toward the roof of the tent. "It's nothing like what you do, though. Your show . . . it's, well, my knot is nothing like that!"

"Do you really think so?" the Lightbender asked. "I'm not sure I agree."

"It's only a little thing," said Ephraim. "What you do is . . ." He spread his arms as wide as he could to indicate the whole of the tent and the circus and the world beyond it.

"Just because a magic is small doesn't mean it is unimportant," the Lightbender said. "Even the smallest magics can grow."

They talked until it was almost time for Ephraim to leave once and for all. It didn't make much sense, but as the minutes passed, he could *feel* his ticket expiring. It felt like being slowly muffled over in layers of cotton. Eventually, it became too uncomfortable for him to ignore.

"I've got to go."

The Lightbender nodded. "Yes, I know. It's time."

They stood and shook hands again. Then, a strange expression crossed the Lightbender's face, as if he'd had an idea that was unexpected but not entirely unpleasant. "Ephraim," he said in a measured voice, "would you like me to give you a miracle?"

"Yes," said Ephraim, which is the only answer anyone should have to that question.

"Anything," said the Lightbender. "As long as it is within my power. What would you like?"

Ephraim was on the verge of asking to have his father back home from the war right then, that very minute. Maybe the Lightbender could make the army think that

his father was injured, or he could make them forget that
there had ever been a Corporal Tuttle at all. He opened his
mouth.

And shut it again.

His father's one letter home had said that what he was
doing in the war was very important, even if it kept him
away from his family. It said he had already saved someone's life. It said that people needed him.

But I need him. Mother needs him.

Ephraim remembered that beautiful vision the Lightbender had shown him. He could have that. All he had to
do was ask for it.

"I want . . ." Two different Ephraims were fighting to
use the same mouth. *My father,* said one of them. *To do the
right thing,* said the other. He was breaking right down the
middle.

Father would want me to do the right thing, he thought.
Even if it hurts. He breathed the disappointment in and
out a few times to see if he could live with the taste of it.

He would have to think of another miracle.

"Trouble choosing?" asked the Lightbender. He sounded
surprised.

Ephraim nodded glumly. "I don't suppose I could save
it for later?"

"It's a miracle." The Lightbender tilted his head and
squinted one eye as if he were trying to figure out what
kind of creature Ephraim might be. "It doesn't expire."

"Oh!" Ephraim guessed that that made sense. "In that case I'll keep it for some time when I really need it. Thank you very much."

Now that the decision was made, he became aware that the cottony feeling of his ticket running out was becoming a suffocating feeling. His time was up. Ephraim hurried to the door of the tent, and just as he reached it, he found the last bit of his courage. He looked back at the Lightbender.

"You've *changed* me."

16
THE PHOTOGRAPH

"Are you sure you didn't write the message yourself somehow? Or imagine it?"

Micah slapped his hand against the quipu's poster board and glared at Jenny. "You're just being stubborn!"

They were standing at the base of the oak tree, loading Jenny's things into her bike wagon. "How could I imagine something like that?"

"You could have dreamed it?"

"In the middle of class!"

"We did stay up really late last night."

The suggestion sounded halfhearted at best. Jenny refused to believe that the wind Micah had felt and the arrow in his notebook and the message the quipu had spelled out were magical phenomena, but she was having a hard time coming up with explanations for what else they could be. She also couldn't deny the fact that the wind had started blowing outside just as Micah saw the message, and it hadn't stopped since. It was more of a normal wind than a gale now, but it was undeniably followable.

"Let's just . . . not argue about it anymore, okay?" Micah dropped *The Big Book of Big Tops* into the wagon. "What is this thing anyway?"

"It's Watson's Pooch Prowler," Jenny said, as if that should make perfect sense. Then she saw the expression on Micah's face and giggled. "Watson's my mom's German shepherd. They go everywhere together."

She flipped up the bike's kickstand. "I'm sorry I can't stay longer. My parents will worry. But are you *sure* you don't want me to tell your aunt that you didn't have anything to do with the feathers?"

Micah shook his head. "I'll stay out of her way."

Jenny's smile drooped a little. After a moment of awkward silence, she said, "Sooo . . . what *are* we going to do about the message?"

"I'm going to do what it says of course."

"I know but . . ." she trailed off.

"I'll tell you all about it tomorrow," Micah promised. "If you want me to, I mean. I'll tell you about the Lightbender and the Bird Woman and the Strongmen and everything else."

Her eyes widened. "You're going to go *without* me?"

Micah had thought she understood. "I have to go tonight, Jenny. The quipu said midnight. I think that's when the circus will open. Grandpa Ephraim can't wait any longer."

One of Jenny's hands went to a braid and started to pull at it. "I know that," she said. "That makes sense, but . . ."

"But what?"

She frowned. "I . . . I can't let you go alone. It was like an adventure we were having together. I'll go with you."

He shook his head. "Your parents."

Jenny drew herself up to her full height. "I'll sneak out of the house." She said this the way other people might announce their intention to dismantle a bomb.

Micah gaped at her.

She threw her leg over the bicycle seat. "I'll be back at eleven o'clock," she said firmly. "Call me if the plan changes. My phone number is 555-3612. It's simple to remember because the numbers double—three, six, twelve."

Before Micah could say anything else, she pedaled away.

Avoiding Aunt Gertrudis on the way in turned out to be easier than Micah had thought it would be. She was in the kitchen, talking on the telephone with Dr. Simon.

". . . gave my brother an extra dose," she was saying. "For all the good it did. That boy won't let him have a moment's rest. Did I tell you I found feathers all over the place? Completely unsanitary . . ."

Micah hurried upstairs before he could hear anything

else. He dropped the quipu on top of his bed, and then he went straight to Grandpa Ephraim's room. The window was open, so the room was bright, and it smelled fresher than usual. But to Micah's disappointment, his grandfather's eyes were closed. He crept closer to the bed. If his grandfather's breath hadn't been gurgling in and out of his chest, Micah would have been terrified.

He looked so much worse than he had two days ago.

Grandpa Ephraim's cheeks were thin and sunken, and they were much too pale. His hands were resting on top of his bedspread. Micah only resisted the urge to reach for one of them by reminding himself that after tonight everything would be better.

Midnight couldn't come soon enough.

His aunt's voice was just a mumble through the floorboards, but as long as he was quiet, he would know when she finished her conversation with Dr. Simon. He unlaced his shoes and slipped out of them so that he could walk on sock feet.

Micah went around the room, looking at the photographs. Every now and then he would tip one a bit to one side or the other to make it crooked. When he did this, the walls looked like Grandpa Ephraim was in charge of them instead of Aunt Gertrudis. Then he reached the corner by the chest of drawers and saw that one of the pictures was already askew.

It wasn't very crooked, but every other frame in the

room had been so perfectly straight that Micah could have balanced a marble on top without worrying that it might roll off. In the photo, a younger Grandpa Ephraim was wearing a gray suit. He had his arm wrapped around the waist of a pretty woman in a polka-dotted dress. She was very small. The top of her head didn't reach Grandpa Ephraim's shoulder. This was Micah's grandmother.

He carefully took the photograph off the nail that held it to the wall. He turned it over in his hands, looking for any clues that might tell him what made it different.

The back of the old wooden frame had a tiny clasp. Micah carefully lifted it with his thumbnail so that he could slip the picture out. The photograph was cool and smooth against his fingers, and as Micah pulled it free, he could see that there was loopy writing on the back of it.

> *Ephraim & Victoria Tuttle in the garden,*
> *photographed by Gertie*

He thought it was wonderful that Aunt Gertrudis had once been nice enough to take pictures of people. He wondered what had gone wrong.

The mattress creaked behind him, and he looked over his shoulder. Grandpa Ephraim was stirring in his sleep. Micah hastily stuck the picture back into its frame.

"Micah?" Grandpa Ephraim sounded groggy.

He rushed over to perch on the edge of the bed. He

reached for his grandfather's hand and held it gently in his own. It was so much thinner and colder than he remembered it being.

"Look at you," said Grandpa Ephraim. His eyes were clear, but his head stayed pressed into his pillows. He didn't lean toward Micah like he usually did. "Growing again. They must be teaching you how to be a giant at school."

It was an old joke they had shared because Micah was short for his age. Grandpa Ephraim used to say it every day when he came home from school.

"I don't think I'm any taller," Micah replied. "But I have learned something important." He bent close to his grandfather's ear. "Circus Mirandus is coming. Tonight. I'm going to get the Lightbender for you."

Micah hated to admit it, even to himself, but a part of him was disappointed that this news didn't make Grandpa Ephraim leap from his bed with joy.

"Tonight, is it?" he asked. "You'll have to make sure you see everything for me. And say hello to the elephant. We always got along well."

"I'll have time for that later," Micah said. "First we have to get the Lightbender to come for you."

Grandpa Ephraim sighed. His eyes held Micah's. "Promise me you'll see some magic tonight. Promise me you won't let worrying get in your way. If you just go, my miracle will take care of itself."

"But . . ."

"Promise me." His voice was so serious.

"I promise," Micah said reluctantly.

His grandfather gripped his hand tighter. "I want you to have something. For luck."

He nodded toward the bedside table, and Micah opened the top drawer. Inside were a Bible, two neckties, tarnished silver cuff links, and one long, dirty bootlace.

Micah's breath caught at the sight of the lace. His fingers hovered over it. "Are you sure?"

"It's waited a long time to go back to Circus Mirandus."

The bootlace wrapped several times around Micah's wrist, and it was rough and leathery against his skin. He knotted it carefully with his free hand.

"A nice strong Tuttle knot," Grandpa Ephraim said approvingly. "I couldn't have done it better myself."

He hesitated then, as if he wanted to say something important and couldn't decide whether he should or not. Micah leaned toward him, but Grandpa Ephraim shook his head. "Tell me about the last couple of days," he said. "What have you been up to?"

Micah thought of his quipu and of the wind. He thought of spending the night in the tree house because Aunt Gertrudis had kicked him out.

"I've got a friend," he said.

Grandpa Ephraim's smile stretched across his whole face. "Do you?" he asked. "Tell me about him."

"He's a girl."

"Oh really?"

Grandpa Ephraim waggled his eyebrows, and Micah

snorted. "Noooo," he said. "She's a *friend*. Her name's Jenny Mendoza, and she's the smartest person in the whole fifth grade."

"She must be if she's friends with you."

Micah told him all about the project and Jenny coming over to help finish it. He tried to make it sound like they had spent all night in the tree because it was an interesting thing to do. He could tell Grandpa Ephraim didn't believe him by the way that his eyes narrowed.

"Anyway," Micah said hastily. "Jenny's coming with me tonight. She's going to help me get to Circus Mirandus."

Grandpa Ephraim's noisy breathing paused for a second. "You're taking her with you?"

"She doesn't live far from here. I'll keep her safe."

Grandpa Ephraim's lips twitched up at the corners. "I'm sure you will. And I'm sure I won't ever mention your friend's escapades to her mother and father." He paused. "But, Micah, have you considered that the circus might not be the right place for her?"

Micah frowned.

"She sounds a little . . . rigid," Grandpa Ephraim said carefully. "And Circus Mirandus is not a rigid sort of place."

"She's my friend," said Micah.

Grandpa Ephraim searched his face. He nodded slowly. "You just be yourself tonight, Micah. Who you are is more than good enough."

Before Micah could ask what he meant, the mumble of Aunt Gertrudis's voice downstairs stopped.

"I think that's your cue to leave," said Grandpa Ephraim. "Best not run afoul of her when you've got such big plans in the works."

Micah agreed wholeheartedly. He slid off the bed and bent down to grab his shoes. He was just standing up when he saw the feather. It was a red so bright that it almost made his eyes water, and it was lying on the floor at the corner of the bed's footboard. There was no way Aunt Gertrudis could have missed it when she cleaned the room that morning. Micah grabbed it.

"Has Chintzy been back already?" he asked as he twirled the pristine feather between his fingers. "Why? What did she say?"

"It's nothing to worry about." The expression on his grandfather's face was strange. "She just had some questions for me."

Micah hesitated. "I don't understand . . ."

"It's fine, Micah. I promise."

Footsteps were coming up the stairs.

"Hurry," Grandpa Ephraim said. "Go."

Micah went.

CHINTZY'S NEWS

Circus Mirandus had rarely been as stirred up as it was on its first night in Peal. Most of the performers still didn't know why they had been dropped onto a new continent so unexpectedly, and the manager was endlessly calling staff meetings to keep everyone up-to-date. Tents had to be set to rights, and schedules had to be rearranged, and of course there was the usual kerfuffle with the menagerie, because no matter how many times they'd done it, the animals still thought that traveling by Door was a rotten idea.

Chintzy was busy as well. When she wasn't zipping here and there with messages, she was trying to convince everyone to use "Lightbender," even though the Man Who Bends Light was being stubborn about the new name.

The *Lightbender* was trying to put his tent in order when Chintzy flew in to share the latest news. Because of the sudden move, his books were scattered everywhere, his clothes were strewn all over the floor, and Chintzy's perch was missing. She sat on top of his dressing table while he stalked back and forth amid the wreckage.

"It was Victoria," Chintzy squawked. "In the picture on the old man's wall. He didn't want to talk about it, but it was her."

"That is impossible," he said. "It doesn't make any sense. How could Ephraim possibly know her?"

"I'm not a liar!"

"I never called you one." He picked up a lantern, looked at it with a vacant expression, then set it back down in exactly the same place. "But it doesn't make sense."

"That's not all." She bobbed up and down eagerly.

He didn't look at her. "Did you deliver the message to Ephraim?" he asked. "Did you tell him—"

"I *told* him," Chintzy squawked. "Did you hear me? I said *that's not all.*"

"All what?"

She hissed at him. "That's not all about *her.* There's more."

He tossed his hands up into the air. "I cannot worry about her. Not today. Not right now."

"That's new."

He glared at her. "If you are not careful I will make you look and sound and smell like an *ostrich* to everyone for an entire week."

Chintzy froze. "You wouldn't."

He started stacking books on the shelves.

Chintzy shuffled back and forth on the dressing table until she thought she might explode. "It's important!" she burst out. "I don't care if you turn me into an ostrich."

The Lightbender sighed, and his shoulders hunched. "What?"

"In the picture, she was wearing a dress with spots on it," Chintzy said darkly.

"Is that significant?"

"She was wearing a *dress*."

The Lightbender had the nerve to look confused. "Victoria was, or is, a girl. They do things like that."

"It was a pretty dress and he was in a suit and they were standing very close together." Chintzy nodded sagely.

But the Lightbender still looked baffled. She decided she had better spell it out for him. "I suspect," she said, "that they might have hatched eggs with each other."

He stared at her for so long that Chintzy thought he was having trouble coping with the gravity of the situation. She started sorting through the things on the dressing table with her beak to see if he had any smelling salts lying around, but then a sound came out of him that stopped her in her tracks.

That horrible Lightbender, that wretched magician, was laughing his head off.

She had never seen anything like it. He almost never laughed, and now he was actually clutching at the shelves for support while he cackled like a madman. He'd obviously cracked under the pressure of the last few days. "I'm serious!" she shrieked.

"I am so sorry," he gasped between chuckles. "I know you are."

"Micah Tuttle might be Victoria's grandchick!"

That sobered him up. "He might," he conceded. "But it hardly matters right now. We haven't even met the boy yet."

"It will matter to the Head! You know it will."

"Not as much as you think," he said. He caught her doubt-filled eyes with his own. "Let's not mention it to him just yet, though."

"I can keep a secret. The Head was too busy to listen to me anyway. But no more laughing!" She snapped her beak at him. "I don't understand why you thought it was funny."

He held one hand over his mouth to hide what Chintzy was sure was an inappropriate grin. "My dear parrot, I have to tell you, human children don't hatch out of eggs."

THE AMAZING
AMAZONIAN BIRD WOMAN

Victoria Starling was thirteen years old when her father's third insanity came upon him. Kinder individuals might have called the third insanity a moment of divine inspiration, or simply a change of heart, but Victoria's mother had been married to Mr. Starling for two legitimate insanities. She wasn't inclined to take the more charitable view.

Victoria herself was never charitable. She thought it was a tremendous waste of effort.

The first insanity had begun just after the Starlings were married, and it involved an obsession with millinery, which is a fancy word for hat making. Mr. Starling quit a lucrative career in banking in order to make flowery ladies' hats.

They were all quite ugly, and after his retirement, a certain museum kept the collection in storage so that they might bring it out during one of those dry spells when people grew tired of seeing Egyptian sarcophagi.

The hat insanity ended just after Victoria's birth, and the second insanity began. Mr. Starling moved his family to the Untamed Wilds of Canada in order to take up a career as a furrier, which is a fancy way of saying that he ran about the woods conking small animals on the head and peeling their skins off.

Mr. Starling was better at conking and peeling than anyone else. He made a great deal of money, and his daughter enjoyed every luxury a young girl could possibly want. Mr. Starling had gowns and chocolates and porcelain dolls shipped in by the truckload. But Victoria was never quite satisfied with these offerings. What good were fine gowns if there was no one around to be jealous of how lovely you were in them?

She craved the admiration of others, and that was in short supply in the Untamed Wilds. Victoria felt certain that she was destined for somewhere much more unusual and glamorous.

Her father's third insanity was a tremendous disappointment.

It came in the night and drove Mr. Starling out of bed. He woke his wife and daughter to announce that he was determined to be a missionary to tribes of heathens living in the Amazon rain forest. He was sure these tribes existed in untold numbers and that they would greet him with open arms.

Mrs. Starling and Victoria protested at extraordinary length and volume, but Mr. Starling would hear none of it.

"I've found my true calling, darling," he said to his wife. "Aren't you happy for me?"

She burst into tears.

Mr. Starling reminded her that she hadn't been all that excited about Canada, either.

The third insanity took off at record speed. Mr. Starling sold his furrier business for bottom dollar and informed his wife and daughter that they would be allowed only one suitcase each for the journey, since they would be dedicating themselves to a life of poverty.

Then Mr. Starling made his fatal mistake. Instead of traveling by ships or trains like a normal man of the times, he decided to call in a favor from a friend who had an airplane. The airplane would have to make stops along the way, but it would get them started on their missionarying faster than anything else.

"I won't do it!" Mrs. Starling cried. "I won't go up in one of those newfangled contraptions. I won't!"

Mrs. Starling said, "I won't, I won't!" until the day arrived and she was stuffed along with her gigantic suitcase into the tiny plane.

For her part, Victoria didn't say much at all. She had never experienced one of her father's insanities before. It was a lot like being struck by lightning out of a clear sky.

At first, she was too baffled by the turn her life had taken to be angry, but that began to change when she saw the plane.

"You're not serious?" she said flatly. It was the first time she had spoken in days. "I won't be subjected to this nonsense!"

"It's perfectly safe, sweetheart," said the pilot, shoving her in beside her mother. "I've flown this beauty four or five times, and it's never failed me once."

Unfortunately for the Starling family, the fifth or sixth time didn't go so well.

When Victoria stopped sobbing, the first thing she noticed was that falling was taking her much too long. Propellers, suitcases, parents—these had all dropped at more or less the same speed toward the earth so very far below her. But judging by the sun, that had been hours ago.

She was a well-educated girl, and she knew such a thing shouldn't be possible.

All of this, from the very beginning, had been a horrible dream. The thought filled Victoria with determination. If she could pinch herself hard enough, she would wake up safely on the ground, at home in her beautiful fur-covered bed, and everything would be back to normal.

She pinched the inside of her elbow until her skin bruised. Victoria stared at the bruise, and the longer she stared the more furious she became. How could her parents have put her in this situation? How could they have died in such a horrible, ridiculous way?

Selfishness. That was the answer. Her father had wanted to be a missionary, of all things, when his daughter was clearly made for something greater. And her mother hadn't protected her from the madness. They had failed to recognize how special she was.

Look at me now, she thought. *I'm not falling to the dirt like some pathetic regular person. I am remarkable. How dare they refuse to see it?*

She wanted to scream. Her parents had gotten it all wrong. The only way to prove how unforgivably wrong they had been about everything was for Victoria to do it all the correct way. She would be rich. She would be famous. She would be powerful.

She pointed her face toward the south and started to fly.

Over the course of the next few months, Victoria Starling wandered in search of fame and glory.

At some point, she discovered a gift for singing. All manner of birds flocked to her, mesmerized by her voice, and she kept a collection of her favorites as pets. Though her talents were substantial, she soon realized that opportunities to show them off were not. County fairs and traveling sideshows provided her with just enough food and shelter, but they weren't what she'd had in mind when she set out. And it was difficult to find money for things like soap, never mind fur coats.

Sometimes, Victoria had the terrible thought that she was starting to look *bedraggled*.

But her luck changed that winter. She was flying away from an unusually grimy traveling fair when she looked down and spotted Circus Mirandus. Victoria could almost feel the magic radiating through the air, and she knew that this was it, the place that was meant for her. She flew right up to the manager's tent and introduced herself as the Amazing Amazonian Bird Woman. She asked about a job.

Requests like Victoria's came along every century or three. People with strong magic were few and far between, and Circus Mirandus held a great appeal for such gifted individuals. Mirandus Head considered each and every one with extreme care, and usually his decisions were made easily enough. Victoria's case posed an unusual difficulty, though.

The manager and a few of his top performers watched her audition in the main tent with a growing feeling of unease. She was as graceful in the air as a swallow. She sang like one of the angels. But her personality—well, it left something to be desired.

Circus Mirandus was in the business of nurturing magic in the world. The performers were inspirers of children. It was a calling that required a special sort of person, and if he was honest with himself, Mr. Head had to admit that Victoria didn't really fit the description. She was volatile and inexperienced, and she was entirely convinced of her own importance.

She was also fourteen years old. How could he leave her to fend for herself?

She landed before him in a cloud of sawdust. Her hands were on her hips, and she was smiling brightly. "Well?" she said. "It's a pretty fantastic show. I'm sure you agree. So do we have a deal?"

He might have said no. He was about to say no. He couldn't risk Circus Mirandus's mission on someone as proud and untried as Victoria Starling.

But one of the performers, one who had been watching from his own private patch of shadow, spoke up. "She's just a girl."

The shadows fell away from the Man Who Bends Light as he approached the manager. "I can keep an eye on her," he said.

If anyone else had made the offer, Mirandus Head would have rejected it.

The Man Who Bends Light was not anyone else.

19

INDEFINITE INVITATIONS

Just after eleven o'clock that night, Micah stood on the sidewalk in front of his house. He was wearing his grandfather's bootlace for luck, and he had freed the quipu from its poster board and stuffed it into his coat pocket, also for luck. He was crossing his fingers and his toes while he waited for Jenny to arrive. It was the kind of night that seemed to require good fortune in the largest possible amount.

The temperature had dropped since earlier in the day, and Micah breathed puffs of fog that only survived for an instant in the steady breeze. He kept one eye on the upstairs windows, in case Aunt Gertrudis woke up and decided to look outside, and the other eye on the empty street in front of him. The parked cars were dark and quiet. Most of the neighbors' houses were too.

He had managed to get his bicycle out of the garage that afternoon without his aunt noticing. It had been several months since he'd ridden it, and the tires were half flat. He didn't know how far they would have to ride tonight. Following the wind sounded exciting and all, but he couldn't help thinking that, as far as directions went, it was a little vague.

Micah heard Jenny coming before he saw her. The Pooch Prowler rattled as it bounced down the sidewalk. She was wearing her bike helmet, jeans, hiking boots, and a dark jacket. Her hair was in one thick braid instead of two. Micah suspected this outfit was the Jenny version of battle armor.

"Are you ready?" she asked when she reached him.

There was a bit of a tremble in her voice, but Micah decided not to mention it as he climbed onto his own bike. He licked his index finger and held it up to the wind the way he'd seen people do in movies. "It's blowing that way."

"This is so crazy," Jenny muttered. "So, so crazy."

Only a couple of cars passed them as they headed downtown, and Micah was glad the streets were quiet tonight. The last thing they needed was a concerned adult stopping to ask them questions.

They didn't talk much while they rode. Micah wasn't sure what Jenny was thinking about, but his own thoughts were a jumble of hope and worry. What if the wind stopped?

What if it didn't, but it led them on and on until morning? What if Aunt Gertrudis or Jenny's parents realized they were missing?

They paused twice to check the wind's direction and readjust their course. As they set off the second time, Jenny cleared her throat. "Micah, if this circus is really here—"

"It's here."

"I was just going to say that if it is, I think I know where it will be."

Micah looked at her. Her expression was equal parts thoughtful and worried. "Where?" he asked.

"There's only one place big enough for a circus in this part of town," she said. "Do you remember last week—"

Micah caught the idea. "They flew those balloons," he said. He should have thought of that himself. The weatherman had mentioned it just yesterday morning. "For the grand opening—"

"Of the new recreation department complex," Jenny finished. "If a whole circus is around here somewhere, that's the only place for it to be."

Micah mulled over the thought as they pedaled past the lightless windows of houses and offices. He knew Circus Mirandus didn't necessarily have to follow normal rules about space. His grandfather's descriptions told him that much. But why wouldn't they take advantage of a large open area whenever they could?

"If it's not at the new rec department," said Jenny hesitantly, "I think maybe we should go back home."

"I can't go back home. Not until I find the Lightbender."
He wouldn't go back even if he had to ride until his
bicycle's wheels fell off.

"Micah . . ." she trailed off as they reached a crosswalk.
They waited for the WALK sign even though there wasn't
a car in sight. The Peal Recreation Fields were just ahead.

Micah eyed the entrance, and his hopes dissolved. It
looked spitefully boring. Scruffy privacy hedges separated
it from the street, and a huge sign with block letters gave
directions toward the parking lot. When they turned into
the main drive, the ball fields stretched out before them
like a quilt.

This doesn't look right, Micah thought. *This doesn't look
like anyplace special.* It even smelled unmagical, like grass
and paint and fresh asphalt. He peered ahead, aching to
spot anything out of the ordinary, but the short grass was
broken only by fences, light poles, and . . .

"Holy smokes," said Jenny.

They coasted to a stop. Giant balloon creatures loomed
eerily in the moonlight. Each one was a sport mascot that
had flown high over the new complex last week to mark
the grand opening. They had been visible from halfway
across town. Now they were tethered to the ground with
ropes and stakes in a field that was probably going to be
a baseball diamond when the recreation department got
rid of the King Kong–sized inflatable gorilla in the out-
field. There were a wasp and a bear and a man who Micah
thought might be a soldier of some kind, but the gorilla

was the biggest. Four thick ropes anchored him to the ground.

"I guess they're keeping them around for publicity," Jenny said. "Or maybe they want to fly them in the May Day parade."

Micah gazed up at the balloons. The quiet of the empty fields pressed against his ears until, as though it had been waiting for the perfect moment, a sound wove its way into his awareness. He shut his eyes and concentrated. It was faint and distant at first, but it seemed to grow stronger the longer he listened.

It was music. It was pipes and drums.

"Do you hear that?" he asked Jenny.

She shook her head. "I don't hear anything."

"It's the music! The music Grandpa Ephraim heard." Micah could feel it now, pulling him toward it. "You were right, Jenny! They *are* here."

Jenny frowned down at the pavement, and Micah knew she was listening with all her might. "Well . . ." she said. "Not really. Where do you hear it?"

They parked the bicycles by the concessions stand, and Micah led the way.

Micah had thought seeing the circus for the first time would be astonishing somehow, but it was the most natural thing in the world when it happened. Between one step and the next, he found himself face-to-face with the place Grandpa Ephraim had described to him so many times.

Circus Mirandus had made a spot for itself between two baseball fields, and it seemed right to Micah that it should be there. The tents, the fluttering pennants, the meadow—the circus looked like it had been waiting for him all along.

The wind pushed him forward. The music pulled him forward. He had thought he would have a hard time keeping his promise to Grandpa Ephraim. How was he supposed to enjoy himself when he was on a mission? Now, though, he was full to the brim with the sight of it.

"It's beautiful," he breathed. "Isn't it perfect?"

"What are you talking about?" Jenny said. She was giving him a concerned look. "What's perfect?"

"The circus of course!"

She looked right at the soaring tents. She blinked. "Are you . . . are you feeling all right?"

"You're joking," said Micah. He pointed toward the circus. "Aren't you? Circus Mirandus is here. It's right here just like you said it would be!"

At first, she didn't seem to believe him. She gripped her braid hard, and she stared at where he was pointing until her eyes started to water. "I don't know, I don't know," she said. "This doesn't make sense. You wouldn't lie to me, though, Micah, would you?"

Micah's chest tightened at her frantic tone. "No! No, I promise, Jenny." He grabbed her arm and dragged her forward. "Just a little closer, and I'm sure you'll see. We're just not close enough."

But they were more than close enough for Micah to see it.

"Okay." Jenny's voice turned serious so quickly that he checked to make sure he was leading the right person. "There must be a logical explanation for this."

He could practically see her brain churning.

"Cameras!" she said, snapping her fingers. "I've heard of this. They can make things appear invisible using lots of tiny cameras and screens to reflect a different image."

"Really?" Micah asked. "Maybe that's it."

He kept tugging her forward. If he pulled her all the way into Circus Mirandus, the magic would have to show itself to her. Wouldn't it? *Oh, please let her see it,* he thought. *It's not fair if she can't see it.*

"I must just keep catching it from the wrong angles," said Jenny. They had reached the ticket taker's line. "I'll see it soon."

Understanding struck Micah like a punch to the stomach.

Jenny couldn't see Circus Mirandus because she wasn't looking for Circus Mirandus. She never had been. He stopped walking and turned to her.

"It's not cameras, Jenny," he said.

"What else could it be?"

He took a deep breath. "Do you trust me?"

"Of course I do!"

He looked her in the eyes. "It's magic, Jenny. It's magic. That's why you can't see it. You have to believe me."

She was already shaking her head. "Micah, I can't—"

"Please?" he squeezed her arm even tighter. "Please try to believe."

"But it's impossible!" she cried. "It's ridiculous!"

"Can't you even pretend? Didn't you ever pretend that magic was real?"

Jenny's eyebrows scrunched together in confusion.

"Just pretend for a second," he urged. "Just say, 'It's a magic circus.' Just once." Maybe she didn't have to believe all the way. Maybe believing a tiny bit would be enough.

"It's a magic circus?" Jenny said.

"Like you mean it!"

She scowled at him. "It's a magic circus."

For several long heartbeats, nothing happened. Then Jenny's eyes widened. "Oh," she said. "How . . .?"

With a sigh of relief, Micah pulled her into line. He spied the ticket taker just ahead. It was Geoffrey, who had been there since 500 B.C. He looked just like Grandpa Ephraim had described him, right down to the golden monocle. Micah whispered this to Jenny while they waited.

"It's probably a family-run operation. He'll be the son or nephew of the original one, I imagine."

Micah shook his head and groaned. When he'd said she only had to pretend magic was real for a second, he hadn't really meant it. Grandpa Ephraim had warned him, but he hadn't thought it would be like this. How could she not understand?

"Which is excellent news for you," she said. "It means that whoever the current Lightbender is will probably be related to the old one. He might even have heard of your grandfather from his own predecessor! Wouldn't that be something?"

She was so excited for him that she was bouncing on the balls of her feet. He refused to regret bringing her. She would see once they were inside. It would be impossible for her to ignore the truth forever.

"Comin' in?" said a voice right next to Micah's ear. He jumped. Geoffrey was standing there, blinking at him through his monocle. "Got your ticket?"

"Don't you sell them?" Jenny asked. "Isn't that your job?"

That was when Micah realized that they might have a problem.

You couldn't buy a ticket to Circus Mirandus. It wasn't that kind of place. Micah understood this even if Jenny didn't. She was already arguing with Geoffrey about the definition of the words "legal tender for all debts." Apparently, they were stamped on the five-dollar bill in her hand.

The wind ruffled Micah's hair, and he had an idea. He pulled the quipu out of his pocket and gave it a few shakes so that it untangled itself. He held it out for Geoffrey.

The ticket taker took it and stared at it through his monocle for a long moment. "This isn't a ticket, Micah Tuttle."

Micah's heart stopped. He didn't have anything else that might be a ticket.

"This is an invitation," said Geoffrey.

"How did you know his name?" Jenny said slowly.

"How long is the invitation for?" Micah asked, which seemed like a much more important question.

Geoffrey switched his monocle to the other eye and gave him a searching look. "Indefinitely."

Jenny looked impressed. "You mean it's good forever?"

"Oho," said Geoffrey. "Now look who doesn't know her definitions."

She drew her shoulders back and opened her mouth, but Geoffrey cut her off. "I mean it's good for as long as it's good," he said. "And then it's not."

Micah still wasn't sure what "indefinitely" meant based on their conversation, but he understood that he was being allowed into the circus. He took Jenny's hand and pulled her toward the entrance.

Geoffrey cleared his throat. "Invitation doesn't have her name on it."

He held the quipu up as if to prove it, and Micah gripped Jenny's hand tighter.

"Her name's right there," he said, pointing at the yellow strand that spelled out Jenny's name in their knot alphabet. He knew that wasn't at all what the ticket taker had meant, but he also knew that he wasn't about to leave his friend out here by herself.

"*Hmm,*" said Geoffrey. He peered at the quipu. "If that's how you want to play it."

He stepped aside and made a sweeping gesture with one arm. "Welcome, Micah Tuttle and friend, to Circus Mirandus."

And finally, at long last, Micah stepped into his grandfather's story.

20

CIRCUS MIRANDUS

Micah could see the golden flag at the top of the Light-bender's tent shivering in the breeze, but it might as well have been miles away. Circus Mirandus wasn't the kind of place you could navigate quickly. Magic was everywhere. The air smelled of grass and smoke and chocolate cake. Lights twinkled overhead like extra stars, and children crowded around groups of performers in exotic costumes. The music Micah had heard was still playing, the drums throbbing in time to Circus Mirandus's pulse. He had to struggle not to lose himself in the wonder of it all.

Jenny wasn't faring any better. Almost as soon as they entered, she was distracted by a tent that seemed to be made entirely of silver smoke.

"What on earth?" she muttered as she walked around it, looking for the entrance. "How did they . . .?"

When Micah reached out to touch the smoke, it drifted away from his fingers. "Come on," he said. "We have to go."

Jenny nodded, and they set off again only to pause when they passed a woman in green striped overalls who was handing out different kinds of candy. A flock of children had surrounded her. Most of them were chewing on jelly cubes that lit up whenever they bit down on them, and the candy glowed right through the skin of their cheeks. One girl had so many stuffed in her mouth that she looked like she was trying to swallow a strand of Christmas tree lights.

"Want one?" the candy lady called to Micah and Jenny.

They did of course, but she didn't wait for them to tell her so. She sent two of the cubes spinning up into the air, and they raced toward Micah and Jenny like comets. Micah caught the orange one, and Jenny caught the pink.

Jenny examined hers like she was trying to turn her eyes into microscopes, then popped it into her mouth. Her cheeks lit up. "It tastes like rose petals," she mumbled thoughtfully while she chewed.

Micah wrinkled his nose. "I'm sorry."

"I like it."

Micah nibbled his own as they headed deeper into the circus and found that his was mango-flavored. *Like the ones Grandpa Ephraim tasted*, he reminded himself. He had to stay on track.

They wove their way through a crowd of children who

were watching a man on a stage put on a funny play. All
by himself.

First he was a baker in a chef's hat and coat. Then, in the
time it took to blink, he transformed into an old lady with
a crooked spine, ordering a cake for her "beloved Jojo's"
birthday. Then he shrank down to become "beloved
Jojo," who was a white rat the size of a watermelon. All
of these changes happened so quickly that Micah couldn't
follow them.

He took another bite of his candy and shook his head.
"Come on, Jenny."

They moved more quickly as they approached their goal,
and they were only distracted for a moment by a swarm
of glittering fairies and butterflies. Dozens of them flitted
past Micah's nose, and when he looked closely, he realized
that it wasn't butterflies and fairies together. It was a group
of fairies that could turn into butterflies. Their wings
hummed in the night air.

They darted toward Micah and then away again, as
though they were trying to tease him into following them.
He smiled, remembering that Grandpa Ephraim had done
just that.

"Sorry," he said. "I've got somewhere else to go."

The Lightbender's tent appeared around the next bend.
It was black with a pattern of gold suns, and it was in the
quietest part of the circus they had been to so far. No other
children stood near the tent, and if not for the distant

shouting and laughter, Micah might have thought the circus was closed. It seemed like there ought to have been more fanfare surrounding the place he had wanted to see for so long.

A Strongman with a bowler hat stood guard over the tent. He was bare-chested except for a pair of suspenders, which Grandpa Ephraim had never mentioned. Micah guessed it was hard to find shirts that fit if your shoulders were as wide as Aunt Gertrudis's old Buick.

He and Jenny walked up to the tent to read the sign next to the entrance. The next showing for the Man Who Bends Light wasn't until 2:00 A.M.

"So late," Micah groaned.

"So early," Jenny corrected.

The dark entrance to the tent had a bright golden rope hanging across it. Micah thought it looked like it would be easy to slip underneath, but then he glanced at the guard. The Strongman tipped his bowler hat down over his eyes and shook his head once.

"I need to see him right away, though," said Micah. "I think I have an appointment?"

The Strongman didn't reply. He also didn't move away from the entrance.

"It's not that long of a wait," Jenny said. "Don't you want to see anything else?"

Micah *didn't* want to see anything else, but he also didn't want to get into an argument with any of the circus people when he was trying to make a good impression. He remembered that Grandpa Ephraim's second favorite part of Circus Mirandus had been the flight show.

He took a tentative step closer to the Strongman. "Excuse me," he said as politely as he could. "Where's the Bird Woman's tent?"

The Strongman slowly pushed his bowler hat back up and stared. "What do you know about the Bird Woman?"

Micah thought it sounded like a trick question. "My grandfather came to Circus Mirandus when he was my age. He liked her show."

The Strongman didn't seem to need to blink. "Victoria," he said. "The Bird Woman. She left."

A jolt of electricity crackled up Micah's back. But Victoria was a common name, he reminded himself. Of course it was just a coincidence.

"Oh." He couldn't imagine why anyone would want to leave this place.

"You're the Tuttle boy," the Strongman said.

Jenny turned to Micah. "The man at the gate knew your name, too. Why does everyone know your name?"

Micah didn't have an answer for her. He had thought that the Lightbender would be expecting him, because of Chintzy, but not everyone else. He held out his hand to the Strongman. He wasn't sure he wanted to shake hands with someone who might accidentally squash him, but the importance of good manners was the only thing Grandpa Ephraim and Aunt Gertrudis had ever agreed on.

"I'm Micah."

A calloused hand four times as large as Micah's shook his gently. "Geoffrey should have told you to stop by the menagerie," said the Strongman. "The manager wants to have a look at you."

MR. HEAD'S
MENAGERIE

·FISH·

Mr. Head's menagerie was at the center of Circus
Mirandus in the largest tent of all. The entrance
was extra-wide, as if it had been made for things much
bigger than humans, and the air around it smelled sweet
and warm. Micah stood outside for several minutes,
trying to muster his courage.

He had thought endlessly of the Lightbender over the
past few days, but the manager of Circus Mirandus hadn't
crossed his mind. Grandpa Ephraim had never said much
about the menagerie or about Mr. Head, and Chintzy had
only mentioned him in passing. Now that he was facing
this imposing tent, Micah wondered if he should have
asked more questions.

Mr. Head is the Lightbender's boss, he realized. *What if he doesn't like me?*

"I've never been to a zoo before," Jenny said. She sounded eager. "My dad thinks they're cruel. But since we're here . . ."

She led the way for a change.

Mr. Head's menagerie was definitely not a zoo. Or maybe it *was* a zoo, but the kind where all of the animals were magical in some way, and free from their cages, and very friendly. A hundred strange smells tickled Micah's nose, and twice as many strange noises pressed against his ears. He could hardly take a step forward without running into a creature more peculiar than any he had ever imagined. Some of the animals had their own habitats, like the miniature hippopotamus in his mud wallow or the bright blue bats hanging upside down from stalactites on the tent's ceiling, but most of the creatures roamed.

Jenny ran from animal to animal, petting them and feeding them from the buckets of treats that hung from pegs on the walls. Micah couldn't keep up with her. He didn't know where to look first. Two long-haired goats and an iguana shared a magazine near the hippo's wallow while the iguana flipped the pages with its tongue. A girl wearing a raincoat was riding on the back of a two-headed camel. Birds zoomed and twittered overhead, pausing from time to time to rest in one of the convenient trees that ringed the edges of the tent. A tiny gray one landed on Micah's shoulder, turned into a mouse, and scrambled down his clothes onto the ground.

As he wandered the menagerie, Micah had the feeling that he was being watched. He looked around for the observer, but it was hard to find something out of the ordinary in a place where *everything* was extraordinary. Micah tried to ignore the creeping sensation, but it grew as he explored the tent. He had almost made up his mind to leave when he spotted the menagerie's centerpiece—a giant aquarium with a single silver fish swimming in the clear water.

Micah stepped up to it, and his nervousness evaporated. The plaque on the side of the tank said, *Fish: A rare specimen courtesy of Ephraim Tuttle.* He ran his fingers over the shiny plaque, tracing his grandfather's name. He looked eagerly around for Jenny and spotted her cooing at a wallaby that could burp the Greek alphabet. He waved her over.

"Wow!" she said. "I guess he really did pay to enter with a fish. What an odd thing to do."

Micah wasn't sure what was rare about Fish, except for the fact that he was enormous now instead of tiny. But when he swam by he flipped his tail in a way that might have been recognition.

They admired Fish until a Strongman, this one wearing a bandanna on his head instead of a bowler hat, brought an aqua-colored baby unicorn into the room. Micah wondered why the Strongman looked so nervous. Then the little unicorn made a sweet sound, like chimes, and Jenny's head whipped around.

"It's *precious!*" she squealed.

At least a dozen screaming girls, Jenny in the lead,

dashed toward the unicorn foal. Micah shook his head as they tackled the Strongman and his charge. He might have liked to see the unicorn himself, but he wasn't sure it was safe to be around so many excited girls.

Grandpa Ephraim had asked him to say hello to the elephant, so he went over to her corner of the tent to meet her. Big Jean wore a giant silver medallion on her harness that said she was *The World's Most Intelligent Elephant*, and after seeing her solve a math problem on an elephant-sized chalkboard, Micah believed it. He scanned the tent for any sign of Jenny. An elephant who could do math—surely *that* would be magical enough to convince her. But even though he stood on his tiptoes and craned his neck, he couldn't find her in the crowd.

Something large and warm tapped him on the shoulder. He turned to find Big Jean's trunk an inch away from his nose. She was holding out her piece of sidewalk chalk. Micah glanced at the chalkboard behind her. Jean had written a new math problem, one that involved triangles and about a million more numbers than Micah had ever seen in his life.

She tapped his nose with her chalk and studied him with patient eyes.

"Um," said Micah. "I'm not that good at math. Why don't you show me something else?"

Jean thumped back over to her board and picked up an eraser the size of Micah's head. The impossible problem disappeared in two swipes, and Jean lifted her chalk again.

Quick as blinking, she drew a map of South America. Micah watched while she squiggled in lines for all the countries. In one of them, she wrote PERU. Then she tossed the chalk over her broad rump to Micah.

He managed to catch it before it hit the sawdust. Jean stared at him. Micah stared back.

The girl on the back of the camel was passing by a few feet away. She waved at Micah and shouted something in a foreign language. It sounded like it might be Spanish.

"What?" Micah called back. "I'm sorry! I don't understand."

"You gotta teach her something she doesn't know!" the girl said in English. "In exchange. I taught her a song."

"How do I know what she doesn't know?" But the girl was busy trying to dig one of the mouse-birds out of the hood of her raincoat, and she didn't answer before the camel carried her away.

"Do you know 'Row, Row, Row Your Boat?'" Micah asked Big Jean.

She nodded.

Of course, he thought. *That was too easy.* Micah racked his brain. "Do you know what a quipu is?"

Jean flapped her ears and nodded again.

Micah was stumped. "Do you know how to make Double Chocolate Brownies?" He wasn't sure why he asked, except that he'd thought the circus smelled a bit like chocolate cake earlier. To his relief, Jean shook her head.

Micah stepped up to the board and froze with his hand

lifted. Was it a *pound* of chocolate chips or a *cup*? Grandpa Ephraim's recipe had been taped to the refrigerator for ages, but Micah hadn't seen it since Aunt Gertrudis came to stay.

Jean was watching over his shoulder. She reached out with her trunk and brushed it curiously against his wrist. The bootlace was wrapped around it. Micah smiled.

"I know what I can show you," he said. "Something no other elephant knows."

Big Jean had learned to tie three different knots by the time Jenny reappeared, and Micah had learned quite a lot about the geography of Peru.

Jenny watched Jean coil rope around a rubber ball. "What's she doing?"

The being-watched feeling had faded to the back of Micah's mind while he worked with the elephant, but it returned full force when Jenny distracted him from his lesson. He glanced over his shoulder.

"What are you looking for?"

"Nothing," said Micah. "It's called a Monkey's Fist knot. Sailors use them."

Micah had only shown Big Jean normal knots. He was still worried that he would tie more of the knots that felt like his grandfather if he tried anything fancy. He turned to Jenny. "You were gone for ages."

Jenny frowned. "That pony is precious, but I really don't

think they should dye its hair like that. It can't be healthy."

"Indeed," said a deep voice behind them. "Fortunately, Terpsichore comes by that color naturally, as do most unicorn foals."

Micah turned slowly. He was sure, absolutely positive, that nobody had been standing behind him a second ago, and the man who had spoken was not the sort of person who was easy to miss.

He looked like Santa Claus, if Santa Claus had a buzz cut and sharp eyes and liked to wear his sleeves rolled up to show off his biceps. He had a large tattoo of a compass rose on one arm, and he was carrying two buckets of something that smelled like maple syrup. Big Jean trumpeted with delight when she saw them.

Micah knew at once this must be Mirandus Head. He realized in the same instant that those icy eyes were the ones that had been watching him ever since he entered the menagerie.

He swallowed around a suddenly dry tongue. "I love your circus, sir." He wondered if he should introduce himself, but he didn't see the point. He was pretty sure that the boss of Circus Mirandus already knew who he was.

"I see you've learned a new trick, Jean, old girl." Mr. Head's eyes lingered on the knots the elephant had tied, and then he set down his buckets and turned to face Micah. He didn't smile, but the lines around his eyes softened. "I am fond of it myself."

"You're the owner!" Jenny realized. "I hoped we'd run into you. I wanted to talk to you about your ticket salesman. He was kind of off-putting."

"Oh, really?" One of Mr. Head's eyebrows climbed his forehead.

Micah winced. After everything they had seen, he had thought Jenny would understand.

As the next five minutes passed in an agony of awkwardness, he realized she hadn't understood at all. She meant well. Micah could tell she did. But, even the way she complimented things was all wrong. It was "What a clever trick you've used over here to make this torch look like it's really floating" and "You must have a wonderful team of geneticists working with you to create bioluminescent bush babies."

Micah wanted to sink into the sawdust and disappear. For the first time, he wished his friend wasn't with him. "Jenny," he whispered. "Jenny, please don't . . ."

But she didn't hear him, and it got worse and worse, until a low, deep growl cut her off. That growl was the kind of sound that sliced open the place inside of you that still remembered when humans were on the lunch menu for monsters with ten-inch-long teeth. A white tiger flickered into existence at Mr. Head's side.

Micah stumbled backward until Big Jean's legs stopped him.

Jenny took a few steps back as well. "That's a tiger," she said. "Only . . . it's too big."

Finally, she had said something Micah could agree with, and he wished that he didn't. He could see his own face reflected in the tiger's pale blue eyes.

"Where . . ." Jenny sounded uncertain. "Where did it come from?"

"My geneticists," said Mr. Head in a voice that was almost as dangerous as the tiger's growl, "must be talented indeed to have invented an invisible tiger."

"I . . ." said Jenny. "Why isn't it on a leash?"

The tiger growled again.

"She doesn't mean it!" Micah said. "She's just . . ." *Rigid*, his brain whispered. "She's just having a hard time with all of this."

Mr. Head gave Jenny a long look that Micah couldn't quite decipher. He stroked the tiger behind one furry ear. "Bibi doesn't approve of leashes," he said. "She is the circus's guardian. Not a pet. No danger can make it past her guard."

Bibi licked his palm, and Micah flinched.

"Well, she couldn't do much against an aerial assault," Jenny said thoughtfully. "Unless she can fly, too."

The manager cut his eyes toward Micah. "Don't you and your . . . charming . . . friend have a show to get to?" he asked in a voice that suggested if they didn't, they should find one.

22

OBVIOUSLY VIPS

"**W**hat's wrong?" Jenny asked as Micah dragged her outside.

"Nothing."

"You're upset. Did I do something—"

"I don't want to talk about it," he snapped.

She fell silent, and Micah immediately felt guilty. She didn't understand. Maybe she couldn't. He thought about trying to explain magic to her again, but that would only start an argument. Micah didn't want to fight. Not tonight.

They trudged back to the Lightbender's tent in silence.

"I'm sorry?" Jenny said when they were almost there. "I guess I shouldn't have talked to the manager?"

Micah sighed. "It's just that he's the Lightbender's *boss*. What if he doesn't want Grandpa Ephraim to have his miracle?" *And he was watching me all that time,* he added in his head. *Why was he spying on me?*

Out of the corner of his eye, he saw Jenny's brow furrow. "I'm sure the Lightbender will still come see your grandfather. They came here didn't they? They wouldn't do that for no reason."

That was true, Micah realized. Circus Mirandus wouldn't have come all this way if the Lightbender didn't want to help. He stood a little straighter at the thought. They were almost back to the Lightbender's tent, with half an hour to go before the show. Everything would still work out.

"I could wait outside," Jenny said quietly. "If you don't want me to meet the Lightbender with you."

Micah was tempted to tell her that was a good idea. But Jenny had come so far with him, and she had helped so much.

"Let me do the talking," he said. "Just . . . don't say much at all, okay?"

"If that's what you want."

When they arrived at the black-and-gold tent, the first thing Micah noticed was that the Strongman wasn't alone. Chintzy perched on top of his bowler hat.

"When we have special guests," she chided, "you don't send them away. It's not done. It's not *professional*."

"We don't ever have special guests," the Strongman said. "The Lightbender didn't tell me to let him in early. And didn't Mr. Head want to—"

"Aha!" Chintzy squawked. She had spotted Micah and Jenny. "There you are."

Micah looked up at her. "Hi, Chintzy."

She bobbed up and down. "Hello to you. You've been expected." She jerked her beak at Jenny. "*You* haven't.

"What did you bring her for?" she asked Micah. "She swatted me."

Jenny reached into the pocket of her jacket and pulled out a plastic bag. It was stuffed full of peanut butter crackers. "I brought these in case we saw you again. As a peace offering."

Chintzy craned her neck down over the rim of the Strongman's hat so that she could glare at him. "What's wrong with you? These children are *obviously* VIPs."

She looked sideways at Micah through a beady yellow eye. "The Lightbender wants to talk to you before his show. He wanted to talk to you before you met the Head as a matter of fact, but Bowler here," she rapped the Strongman's hat with her beak, "didn't get the memo."

"Wouldn't that be the messenger's fault?" Jenny whispered under breath. Fortunately, Chintzy didn't hear her.

"Right now?" Micah asked.

The golden rope that hung across the entrance to the

tent dissolved. Chintzy pointed at it with one wing. "What do you think?"

The room Chintzy led them to was obviously where the Lightbender lived, even if it didn't look much like any home Micah had ever seen. A plain four-poster bed was tucked off to one side behind a silk screen, but the rest of the room's contents were less ordinary.

Micah assumed the Lightbender must keep his clothes in the big ironbound chest at the foot of the bed, because there were no closets or wardrobes. The only chair in the room had been pushed under a flowery mirrored vanity that looked more like something Aunt Gertrudis would use than a powerful magician. Beside the vanity, a silver coffee service with a steaming pot teetered on the back of a short table that was shaped a lot like Big Jean. A tall mahogany bookshelf curved around one side of the room. Books, scrolls, lanterns, and maps fought for space on it, and some of them had spilled onto the floor, which was covered in ornately patterned rugs and cushions.

In the midst of it all stood the Lightbender. He looked just like Micah had imagined he would, except for the fact that he was fidgeting with the cuffs of his coat. The coat itself was perfect. The dark brown leather had so many scratches and scuffs on it that Micah knew it must have been part of a hundred adventures. But, he hadn't thought the Lightbender would be the sort of person who fidgeted.

"Ah," he said when they entered. "Micah Tuttle and . . ." He looked curiously at Jenny.

"I'm Jenny Mendoza."

Chintzy flapped to a tall perch beside the elephant-shaped table. "She brought me crackers," she said. "We like her."

The Lightbender nodded as if he agreed that crackers were a good way to determine someone's character. He indicated a particularly thick stack of cushions with a wave of his hand. "I apologize for the lack of chairs," he said, his eyes meeting Micah's briefly before twitching away. "Please have a seat."

Micah and Jenny made themselves comfortable on the floor while the Lightbender busied himself with the coffee service.

"Are you thirsty?"

"No, thank you," Jenny said.

"I'm fine," said Micah.

"Would you like a drink?"

Jenny and Micah exchanged a confused look.

It took a moment for the Lightbender to realize that he had said something that sounded odd. He glanced at them over his shoulder. "In this tent, those two questions are actually quite different," he said mildly. "Would you like a drink?"

"Orange soda?" Micah asked. He and Grandpa Ephraim used to drink it every afternoon when he came home from school, but he hadn't been allowed since Aunt Gertrudis moved in.

When the Lightbender turned back around, he was carrying a cup of coffee and a frosted glass bottle of orange soda. He passed the soda to Micah and settled down on one of the cushions.

Micah stared at the bottle. It was the same brand of soda Grandpa Ephraim always bought, because they liked the glass bottles better than plastic ones. It was icy cold, exactly like Micah preferred it. But the Lightbender had no refrigerator, and he didn't look much like the kind of person who drank orange soda anyway. Jenny was staring at the bottle, too, as if she couldn't quite figure it out.

Micah took a cautious sip. "It's perfect."

"I do try," the Lightbender murmured.

Jenny crossed her hands in her lap and squirmed, but she didn't say anything. Micah guessed she was taking her promise to let him do all of the talking seriously.

The Lightbender sighed. "Unfortunately, our time is not unlimited, and we have much to discuss. Tell me why you've come, Micah. We'll move forward from there."

Micah took a deep breath. *Finally.* This was it. "It's my Grandpa Ephraim, sir. He needs his miracle."

"I know."

Micah nodded. "It's his lungs. I think he would have come to you himself only he's too sick to get out of bed."

He paused to glance at the Lightbender's face and was relieved to see that he didn't look surprised by any of this. "The doctor says he probably doesn't have much time left." Micah swallowed. "So it's urgent."

He stopped speaking. He hadn't said much, but he felt like he'd run a race. Jenny reached out and put a hand on his shoulder.

"What is it that you want from me, Micah? Tell me exactly."

Micah had thought that was really clear, but he answered anyway. "I want you to help Grandpa Ephraim. I want you to stop him from dying."

Jenny made an upset chirping sound then cleared her throat. "Or if you could just come talk to Mr. Tuttle, sir," she said. "To remind him of better times and make him feel more cheerful. He knew one of your predecessors, you see."

Micah shot her the most scorching look he could manage, and she fell silent. He couldn't let this meeting turn out like the ones with Geoffrey and Mr. Head had.

But the Lightbender only wrinkled his nose, as if what she had said smelled funny. "How old are you, Jenny?"

She looked confused. "Almost eleven."

"Tragic," he muttered. He turned back to Micah. "Tell me, how much do you know about your grandfather's time at Circus Mirandus?"

"Everything," Micah said confidently. He held up his

wrist to show the Lightbender the bootlace. "He told me about your show and about Geoffrey and Fish. He told me you promised you would give him a miracle." Micah thought. "And he talked about the Bird Woman."

"Victoria!" Chintzy squawked. "I knew it."

Micah jumped. He had almost forgotten the parrot was in the room.

"Hush," the Lightbender said to her. He looked down at the bootlace with a fond expression on his face. "I remember, of course. Can you perform the same magic with this humble lace that Ephraim could?"

"He taught me the trick," Micah said. "I'm good at it."

For the first time since Micah had entered the tent, the Lightbender truly smiled. "It was right after Ephraim showed me that particular talent that I offered him the miracle."

"I know."

The Lightbender caught Micah's eyes with his own. "I promised him anything within my power."

Micah nodded eagerly.

The Lightbender's face fell. "Perhaps I am going about this the wrong way. Micah—and you too, of course, Jenny—will you please do me the honor of attending my show?"

"But—"

"I think it will make everything much clearer," the Lightbender said.

Micah hesitated. "You *are* going to keep your promise to Grandpa Ephraim, aren't you?"

The Lightbender's fingers tightened around his cup. "I am going to do all I possibly can to fulfill Ephraim's request."

Everything that had been wound so tightly inside of Micah began to uncoil.

The Lightbender cleared his throat. "Let's talk about something else for our last few minutes together, shall we?" he said. "My show has changed a bit in the past decades, but you'll be able to experience many of the same things that Ephraim did, Micah."

"The show," Chintzy muttered from her perch. "He wants to talk about the show."

"Chintzy," the Lightbender said in a warning voice.

"It's absurd!" she squawked. "You might not get another chance to ask him."

"Not another word."

"Ask me what?" said Micah.

The Lightbender and the parrot were having a staring match.

"It's nothing important," said the Lightbender. "Chintzy has been high-strung of late."

Chintzy hunkered down on her perch as if she were settling in for a long sulk, but as soon as the Lightbender turned his back, she squawked, "You know something about Victoria, don't you?"

Micah frowned. "That was my grandmother's name."

"I knew it," Chintzy said.

"But I never even met her," said Micah. "I don't know anything about her at all. Did . . . did you both know her?"

The Lightbender closed his eyes and sighed.

23

THE BIRD WOMAN'S FINAL PERFORMANCE

After wasting almost ten years of her life at Circus Mirandus, Victoria Starling had concluded that children were abominably foolish creatures. Take her younger self, for example. When she had first heard about a circus full of magically gifted individuals, it had sounded like a dream come true. She had been taken in by the grand tents. She had been charmed by the promise of starring in her own show.

She had never been as witless as most children; she had had her ambitions at least. But it had taken her far too long to realize that those ambitions were too small for her. The circus had offered her the trappings of power, and child that she was, she had mistaken them for the real thing.

It hadn't been so bad at first. She did like to perform, and she especially liked to perform better than everyone else. Well, almost everyone else. There was the matter of a certain illusionist, but being just a hair less popular than a magician who had been at the job for centuries was no small feat.

Her shows were masterful, every one of them a unique work of art. As they traveled the world, Victoria had lured more and more birds into her flock, and she had learned how to incorporate them into her routines. She and her flock soared. They danced through the air so flawlessly that even the Strongmen shed an occasional tear.

And her song—no one had ever heard its equal.

Victoria could direct any bird with a few crystalline notes. Her silver swans dipped over the crowd. Her parrots sang arias. Hummingbirds swarmed in glistening clouds. In the center of it all there was Victoria herself, and she knew exactly what those silly little faces saw when they looked up at her so longingly from the ground. A lone spot of white amid a riot of color, a feathered angel.

It was satisfying. She had to admit that.

It was also utterly pointless.

Someone with her skills squandering their time to make a tent full of children, most of whom were unremarkable in every way, happy? It was absurd. The fact that a whole circus full of magicians was dedicated to that goal? Practically criminal.

Once she had finally grown up enough to realize how misguided she had been, Victoria began to withdraw from the other performers. And as she withdrew she saw more and more clearly how useless the circus was. She started taking long flights away from Circus Mirandus. She had heard the Head talk about their purpose a thousand times before—"giving hope" and "fostering belief"—but out in the real world those abstractions weren't making any difference that really mattered as far as she was concerned.

During her outings she kept her ear to the ground, and eventually she began to pick up the sort of information that interested her. Circus Mirandus was by far the largest group of magical individuals in the world, but there were others. And some of those others were concerned with things much more worthwhile than the delicate feelings of children.

With a wider world calling and the other performers constantly nagging her to spend more time catering to the whims of her audience, Victoria made up her mind. She would leave Circus Mirandus, and good riddance. She would have to abandon most of her flock. Traveling with a hundred or so birds wasn't practical, and she could always get new ones. But, if possible, she was going to take one particularly valuable asset with her.

It shouldn't be too hard. He was quite fond of her. After all, they had been friends for years hadn't they? And he was clever. Surely, he wouldn't choose this suffocating old place over Victoria Starling.

The Man Who Bends Light found Victoria in her dressing room. She pulled aside the curtain that served as her door and smiled when she saw him. "I suppose you're here to scold me," she said.

"Are you ill?" he demanded.

"No."

"Are you injured?"

"No."

"Then, yes, I suppose I am here to scold you." He swept inside. "You skipped *three* shows today. Without the slightest warning! Mr. Head is furious."

"Mr. Head is always furious about *something* I've done."

"In this case, it's about something you have *not* done. The children were waiting for ages. One little boy *cried*. Here! At Circus Mirandus. Victoria, what were you thinking?"

She crossed her arms over her chest. She was wearing her costume, which seemed an odd choice to him since she hadn't bothered to work that day. "Don't you ever get tired of it?" she asked.

"Of what?"

"Of the circus. Of all of these silly shows we waste our time on when we could be doing so much more!"

"Silly?" he said. "I have been here for many centuries. Obviously, I do not feel that Circus Mirandus is a waste of my time."

"Clearly you haven't thought about it like I have," she said.

He raised an eyebrow.

"The circus is a fine place," she said, "for some people. But you're different. *We're* different."

"Different?" The Man Who Bends Light drew the word out as though it tasted foul.

If Victoria heard the warning in his voice, she chose to ignore it. "Powerful," she said bluntly. "We can be like gods out there. We can make a *real* difference. Why would we stay here and act as . . . as nursemaids to children who aren't anything special?"

She had been stepping toward him as she warmed to her subject, but she stopped when she saw his face. "You know it's true," she said. "You must have considered it yourself."

"Of course I haven't!" he shouted. "Of all the selfish, ignorant . . . do you really think that you are superior to everyone else? Because you can fly?"

"Not everyone." She smiled at him again.

He took a deep breath to calm himself. "You have always been less than modest about your talents. I had assumed it was a failing of youth."

"I'm not that young anymore," she protested.

"What I cannot comprehend is your inability to appreciate what we do here. Do you *realize* that magic as we know it is fading? Do you realize that Mr. Head, Geoffrey, the Strongmen—all of us!—are fighting to keep enchantment alive in the world? You say the children aren't special, but they are. They are the key to everything. What we do here is *important*, Victoria."

She shook her head.

"Yes," he said. "Not only important, but vital. You are part of something great, and the tragedy is that you don't even see it."

"I see clearly enough," she argued. "What do you know about it? You never go out into the real world. Half of the children don't even remember Circus Mirandus a few years down the road."

"But *some* of them do. It matters. It makes a difference. I am not as ignorant of the world beyond our gates as you seem to believe."

"Are you sure about that?" she said. "Because I've seen them. The children. They leave believing well enough I suppose, but one little accident, one little misstep and—" She snapped her fingers.

"And if they do believe for their whole lives, what of it? They can't do anything useful about it. They just pine after what we have. If you think about it, it's cruel to tease them." She drew herself up to her full height. "I don't want to *waste* myself here. I want . . ."

"Power?" he asked.

"Maybe," she admitted. "Is that so wrong?"

His silence was as good an answer as any.

Victoria huffed a laugh. "Now you've gotten me off track," she said. She picked up an ivory comb from her dressing table and ran her fingers over its teeth. "I didn't want to argue with you. You're my closest friend, you know."

"You are not the easiest person to befriend," he said.

"I'm perfectly lovely, and you know it," she said, pointing the comb at him. "In all seriousness, though, I was hoping you would be the one to come and yell at me for skipping those shows."

The Man Who Bends Light crossed his arms over his chest. "Victoria—"

"Come with me." She leaned toward him. "Let's find others like us. I've got a few contacts, and there must be others out there. You want to make a difference in the world. Well, so do I. Just imagine what we could accomplish together!"

"Dear Victoria," he said. "You are so very young."

She opened her mouth, but he held up a hand to silence her. "If you truly consider me your friend, please listen to me now. I have traveled the world many times over, and I have learned many hard lessons over the years. I would spare you my own mistakes."

He gripped her shoulders and looked into her eyes. "Stay for one more show. Give one final performance. Put everything you have into it, and after it's over, stay a while. Speak to the children. See how you have changed them. *That* is power."

He stepped away from her. "If you don't agree with me, then you can depart, and I hope that we will part as friends."

She stared at him. "I thought you would understand," she said. "You really won't come with me?"

"No," he said. "I won't."

For the first time since he had entered her dressing room, Victoria was at a loss for words. She examined the comb in her hands as though it held a great secret. Then, she shook her head and cast it aside. "One last show," she said. "Don't come. I don't want you there."

The Amazing Amazonian Bird Woman's final show took place on a warm, sunny afternoon, and the crowd was as large as it ever had been, in part because many of her colleagues were in attendance along with the children.

The children had come to see a marvelous show. The other performers had come to bid Victoria farewell. Mirandus Head had come because he was the manager. He watched as she spun through the air so far above the crowd, and he wondered how a person who had been given so much throughout her young life could be so determined to give nothing back.

But even Mr. Head had to admit that the Bird Woman's final performance was going well. She had a way of holding the crowd's attention that was almost unmatched. She soared, white feathers fluttering around her, and the children cried out in astonishment as she swooped low over their heads. When Victoria began to sing, wonder stole across the faces of dozens of boys and girls. Their eyes widened in delight when her flock entered the tent. Several of the children reached up, longing to touch those magnificent birds.

That was when Victoria spoke from high overhead. "Do you like my flock?" she asked in a sweet voice. She stood in the air as though she were standing on a sheet of glass, and the sunshine pouring through the tent's skylight made a halo over her head.

The children cried out with a chorus of yeses.

Victoria held out one hand and trilled a series of diamond pure notes. One of the silver swans swooped toward her. It was a beautiful creature, fatly elegant with platinum wings and a graceful neck. It nuzzled Victoria's hand.

"They're all very rare," she said as the flock circled her. The beat of their wings made her hair whip around her face. "Some of my birds are the only ones of their kind in the entire world."

She stroked the swan's beak. "This one is named Eidel. Would you like to see her up close? I'll need a volunteer."

The tent burst into excited chatter. One little girl raised both of her arms over her head and jumped up and down.

"You in the brown dress," Victoria said, pointing at her. "Come to the center of the floor please."

The girl scampered forward and looked up eagerly at the Bird Woman and the swan.

"Now, don't move," said Victoria. "I don't want you to frighten Eidel."

The girl nodded, and Victoria bent her head to the swan. She cooed gently, and the bird looked down at the girl. It dove. The audience held its breath as the swan fell like a shooting star.

Down, down, down the swan dove.

The girl in the brown dress watched with huge eyes. She was still smiling when the swan broke itself against the ground at her feet.

It hit the floor in an explosion of silver feather and sawdust, and in the half second of silence that followed, the sound of its wings scrabbling against the ground as it died was enough to tear a hole in Mirandus Head's heart.

The girl screamed. She staggered away from the fallen swan.

As though her scream was the signal, the birds in the tent went mad. Some of them pelted toward the earth as the swan had. Others turned on their fellows. The hawks and the eagles ripped into the songbirds, and feathers rained down.

Mr. Head leaped out of the way as a phoenix hit the ground next to him and burst into flame.

"Victoria!" he bellowed. "Stop this!"

The tent was filled with screaming now. It was a nightmare of crumpled birds and fleeing children. In the midst of the chaos, Mr. Head spotted one of the Strongmen shielding a group of children with his broad back. "Get them out of here!" he called. "Clear the tent."

Bibi appeared next to him, roaring loudly enough to rattle skeletons out of their skins, but she couldn't do anything to stop Victoria from the ground. Nor, for that matter, could Mr. Head. They stared helplessly up at her, standing on thin air, and the manager was chilled to his marrow by what he saw in her face.

She did not look furious as she murdered her own companions. She did not look enraged as she terrified an audience full of innocent children. She looked satisfied, as though she had just proven something important to herself and to the rest of the world. He had allowed a monster into Circus Mirandus, and now the children were paying the price.

"DO NOT PANIC!" The voice rang through the tent.

Rang? *No,* ringing was something normal voices could do. This voice pulverized the very air.

The Man Who Bends Light stood in the tent's entrance, and his coat billowed as though caught in a rising wind. "NOTHING IS WRONG."

The children stopped screaming.

Their expressions smoothed into mild curiosity, and they turned to look at him. The birds were still fighting and flailing overhead, but the children, even the ones who had tears running down their cheeks, were suddenly unaware of the chaos. The performers and the Strongmen had been left out of whatever illusion had taken hold of Victoria's audience, but they recognized the Man Who Bends Light's magic for what it was at once.

They leaped into action. They hustled the scratched and bruised audience out of the tent, and within seconds, only the illusionist, the manager, and the Bird Woman were left.

"What have you done?" the Man Who Bends Light asked in a fractured voice. His eyes took in the dead and dying birds that littered the ground. "Victoria, *why*?"

She glared down at him. "I tried to tell you," she said. "One little accident, one little misstep." She spread her arms. "And everything Circus Mirandus works for is destroyed. *Now* do you see how pointless this place is?"

Mr. Head knelt to pick up a dazed bluebird. "As if we did not already know that faith is such a fragile thing," he murmured.

"You should have agreed to come with me," Victoria said to the Man Who Bends Light. She was so bold, so certain that she was far beyond their reach. "You could have been someone who mattered."

Mr. Head knew the moment the Man Who Bends Light made his decision. Resolve replaced the devastation in his features. He strode forward until he stood directly beneath Victoria.

The manager closed his eyes.

"What are you doing?" Victoria sounded more curious than nervous. "I know better than to fall for one of your tricks."

"But you are falling, Victoria," the Man Who Bends Light said in a soft voice. "Did you think you could fly?"

Magic. Faith. Mr. Head thought it ironic that Victoria had never made the connection. Nobody had ever touched magic without believing that they might be able to do so. And very few people could believe in something if the Man Who Bends Light wanted them to think it wasn't true.

Victoria dropped like a stone.

The manager opened his eyes in time to see the magician catch her before she hit the ground. She scrambled away from him as though his touch burned.

"What did you do to me?" she screamed. "What did you do?"

"Such a fragile thing," Mr. Head said quietly. Perhaps the effect would last months, or even years, but Victoria obviously thought it was permanent. She sucked in great gulps of air and stared down at her costume.

"W-what did you d-do?" She choked the words out again between sobs.

"What was necessary," said the Man Who Bends Light. He refused to look at her.

She stumbled to her feet and fled the tent.

"See that she leaves the circus," Mr. Head said to Bibi. "For good."

The tiger growled her agreement and stalked after Victoria.

Mr. Head approached the Man Who Bends Light cautiously. The magician was watching the surviving members of Victoria's flock retreat through the skylight. Every line of his body was etched with grief.

"We should call you the Man Who Bends Minds," the manager said. "I'll admit it's not as cheerful, but it would be more accurate."

"I am sorry." He gave his words to the sky. "I am so, so sorry."

24

THE ILLUSIONIST

The Lightbender led Micah and Jenny into the main section of the tent a few minutes before his show was due to begin. Micah was still clutching his bottle of orange soda. It was as frosty cold as it had been when the Lightbender had first given it to him, but he was feeling so subdued after learning about his grandmother that he had forgotten to drink it. How could he be related to someone like that? How could someone even *be* like that?

And Grandpa Ephraim—how had he even married Victoria in the first place? It sounded like after she left Circus Mirandus nobody knew where she'd gone.

"You might want to finish that now." The Lightbender gestured toward the soda as he ushered them to two front row seats. "I tend to be a little distracted when I am performing. It might disappear on you."

Micah took a big gulp.

Jenny looked around the tent curiously. She examined the stage and the walls. "Do you *really* not use cameras? Is what you do really . . .?" she trailed off, but the word *magic* hung in the air almost as if she had said it aloud.

Micah shot the Lightbender an apologetic look, but he only shook his head at Jenny's question. "You will have to tell me what you think after you've seen it. I do not often perform for children with your particular point of view. The pressure is a novel experience."

He looked up at the ceiling, and the lanterns hanging overhead dimmed as if he had given them a silent command. Micah heard the excited chattering of the children outside increase in volume as the golden rope began to dissolve.

"Thank you," he said. "For telling me about Victoria and for Grandpa Ephraim and for, well, everything."

"Pay close attention to my show, Micah." The Lightbender began to fade into the shadows of the room. "Remember that I promised your grandfather anything within my power."

The frigid air stung Micah's cheeks. He couldn't understand how it was possible. How could he really be standing beside Jenny in Antarctica watching emperor penguins slide down an icy hill on their bellies? But he *was* there. He was so very much there that for a moment he forgot he had ever been anywhere else.

The Lightbender's tent faded from his memory like a dream, and he woke up in a land of ice. Then that became the dream, and he woke up to find that the world was really the sun in his eyes and a crowd cheering and the thunder of racing horses in his chest. That was what the Lightbender's show was like—waking up again and again only to find that every new waking was more perfect than the last.

Micah woke again, this time to find himself deep in the jungle, and he immediately began exploring. He stepped between two bushes with leaves as large as Big Jean's ears and found a twinkling green pool. He drank in the lush sight. Flowering vines swayed over the pool from the branches overhead, and a tiny waterfall splashed down into it from the rocks above. Fish as bright as Easter eggs played among the reeds.

Grandpa Ephraim never mentioned this.

Micah was surprised to realize that he hadn't thought about his grandfather since Antarctica. *The jungle was one of his favorite parts,* he reminded himself. *This is the Lightbender's show. I'm supposed to be paying attention.*

It was more difficult than he had thought it would be to keep that in mind, especially with such a tempting pool right in front of him. Curious, Micah took his shoes off so that he could dip one of his toes in the water. It was just the right temperature for swimming. The moment he decided this, he found that he was wearing swimming trunks.

That's funny, he thought. *Didn't I have on jeans?*

He waded into the cool water, and the fish darted away from him. At its deepest, the pool only came up a few inches over Micah's head. He swam back and forth under the waterfall and dove down to touch the bottom. When he cracked his eyes open and looked up toward the surface, everything was a blur of shimmering color and light. He rose back up again, and shook his head to get the water out of his ears. Droplets flew away from his hair like sparks.

He would have been content splashing around in the tropical forest forever, but eventually the world around him began to change. This time, Micah forced himself to pay attention to the transition. Between one blink and the next, he was standing not in a humid jungle but in a dry and windy desert, and he stared up at a pyramid as tall as a skyscraper.

It wasn't like waking up from a dream this time, maybe because he was trying hard to focus. He was disoriented by the shift. He half expected the blowing sand to stick to him. Surely, he was still wet from his swim.

Only he wasn't wet at all. He was completely dry and wearing a hat with flaps that kept the burning sun from roasting the back of his neck. That was when Micah finally started to understand. That was when he started to worry.

"Anything within my power," the Lightbender had promised. But what *was* the Lightbender's power exactly?

Micah wasn't wet. He never had been, really.

He bent to pick up a handful of sand, and he let it run slowly through his fingers. *It's got to be real.* His thoughts sounded desperate even to himself. *It can't feel like this and not be real.*

Eventually, the pyramid faded out of existence, and he found himself standing at the edge of a lake. It was nighttime, and fireworks exploded overhead. The air smelled like gunpowder.

Micah's hands were empty.

"Usually," said a sad voice, "this is the part where I show you your heart's desire coming true."

The Lightbender appeared beside him. The flashes of light in the night sky painted his face in shadows. "In your case, I fear that is not a good idea."

"You're an illusionist," Micah said. His throat had gone dry.

The Lightbender nodded.

"I knew that. But I didn't realize . . . None of this lasts. It's all in my head?"

"I'm afraid so."

Micah tried to breathe, but he was being crushed from the inside out. "Grandpa Ephraim?" he choked.

"He knows," the Lightbender said softly. He took a step toward Micah. He lifted one arm, as though he planned to reach out to him, but then he dropped it back to his side. "I am sorry."

The fireworks were fading. The Lightbender's tent was coming back into view.

Micah felt like a kite with a cut string, tumbling through the air, the ground falling away beneath him. He barely noticed Jenny trembling in the seat next to him. They were the only children left in the stands.

"He said you could help us, though." Micah's voice was hollow. "Grandpa Ephraim said you could help."

"Not in the way you want me to, Micah. I cannot trick death."

"What good *are* you then?" Somehow, Micah was on his feet. "What good is *any* of this?"

He wanted the Lightbender to argue with him. He wanted him to scream at him so that Micah could scream, too. But the illusionist never raised his voice. "I'm sorry I can't give you what you want. Go to Rosebud. She lives in the wagon behind Mr. Head's tent. She will give you something to make Ephraim feel more like himself, for a little while."

"I don't believe you! You have to be able to help. All of this . . ." Micah waved his arms to encompass the whole of Circus Mirandus. "It's perfect and amazing and . . . and it's *everything*. You can save him somehow. If you would just come back with me, if you saw Grandpa Ephraim, you would help. I know it!"

He shook his head. "I can't, Micah. And I try not to leave Circus Mirandus. I maintain the illusions that keep us hidden from the world. If I leave, things become difficult."

"Please." Micah's voice cracked. "Please come."

The Lightbender looked away.

Micah grabbed Jenny by the arm and pulled her up. He backed away from the Lightbender. "You don't care," he said accusingly. "You're not even going to try."

He tugged Jenny across the stage and toward the exit. His own fury was burning him alive. As he stepped outside, the night air felt like a thousand points of ice against his skin.

In the dark tent behind him, he thought he heard the Lightbender groan. He thought he heard him say something in his too-quiet voice.

"Dear, dear Ephraim. Could you not have asked me for a smaller miracle?"

25

A MITE OF HELP

Micah almost walked into the Strongman on his way out of the tent. The giant in the bowler hat didn't say anything at all. He stepped out of the way and let them pass. Micah bulled his way toward the gate. He wasn't going to spend one more moment in Circus Mirandus than he had to.

Jenny stumbled after him. "Micah," she said in a shocked voice. "Micah, I don't think the Lightbender uses cameras."

"He might as well."

"I . . . I think this . . . All of it is *real*."

Micah snorted.

"Slow down!" Jenny said. "I need a minute. I need to think."

But Micah didn't slow down, and they were just yards away from Geoffrey and the outside world when Jenny dug in her heels. Micah jerked to a stop and dropped her arm.

"What about Rosebud's wagon?" she said.

Micah shook his head. "These people aren't going to help us, Jenny. We shouldn't even have come."

"The Lightbender said she could give your grandfather something to make him feel better, though. If this is all real, don't you want to try?"

No. Micah didn't. He had tried and tried until he was scraped raw inside.

"Micah Tuttle!" Jenny cried. "You can't give up now."

Micah breathed in and out slowly until he had calmed down enough to think. He knew Jenny was right, but vicious disappointment was gnawing its way through his heart. Grandpa Ephraim was going to . . . he was . . . Grandpa Ephraim could use every bit of help Micah could find for him.

"Okay," he said. "Okay."

Micah wasn't surprised that he hadn't noticed Rosebud's wagon before. It looked like a dollhouse next to the menagerie. He didn't want to be too hopeful, but as soon as he saw it, he had to admit that it looked like it had potential. The wagon was painted a bright green that glowed in the light from the spotlight on top of Mr. Head's tent, and four fat yellow ponies were tied to a stake nearby.

The sign beside the three wooden steps that led up to the door said ROSEBUD'S POTIONS AND POULTICES.

"She must be some kind of herbalist," said Jenny. She knocked on the door.

It swung open almost instantly, and they both gasped. The woman standing in front of them was huge. Her skin was as dark as the Lightbender's tent, and she must have been at least seven feet tall. She didn't have a single strand of hair on her head, but her skull was painted with bright pink flowers.

"Um," said Jenny.

"We're looking for Rosebud?" Micah said. "Ma'am."

Her grin was almost as big as she was. "Looking for me?" she said in a booming voice. "Well of course you are, ducklings! Come in."

And before either of them could decide whether that was a good idea or not, she grabbed Micah and Jenny by the shoulders and pulled them into the wagon. Micah wasn't sure, but he thought his feet actually left the ground for a second.

They were dropped onto an armchair so large that it took up almost all of the room in the wagon that Rosebud herself didn't occupy. "Holy smokes," said Jenny.

"I've got those!" Rosebud said. "Is that what you're looking for?"

"No, ma'am." Micah took in his surroundings. A baby alligator with a bandaged tail slept on top of a stack of foreign-language dictionaries and astronomy textbooks in one corner, but every other spare inch of the wagon was covered with jars and bottles and baskets. "At least I don't think so. We're looking for something to fix someone's lungs."

"Oh dear." Her smile faded. "So it's a serious problem you've come to me about? Tell me all about it, ducklings. We'll see what we can cook up."

Rosebud's wagon smelled stranger than any place Micah had ever been, and she wouldn't stop calling him a duckling. But as soon as he finished describing Grandpa Ephraim's symptoms to her, she started reaching into her baskets and beakers and cookie tins, pulling out things that definitely looked disgusting enough to be medicine. "I can't fix everything," she said, "and I can't stop the dying from doing their thing, but this will help a mite."

Jenny whispered into Micah's ear that "mite" meant a little bit, but he couldn't help feeling encouraged while he watched Rosebud grind all of her ingredients with a mortar and pestle that were much too small for her hands. She made a fine, brown powder and tipped it into a small pot with a cork top. Then she dipped a brush into a jar of white paint and wrote, "For Ephraim Tuttle," on it in pretty calligraphy.

"My special tea," she said as she passed it to Micah. "You steep it in some hot water for a few minutes and give it to him. It'll make him feel better."

The pot was heavier than it looked. Micah clutched it to his chest with both hands.

"Thank you," he said. "Thank you so much."

"Aww, duckling." She patted him on the shoulder. "You have a good day."

"Day?" Micah asked. Surely he hadn't been at Circus Mirandus for so long. But when they stepped outside Rosebud's wagon, he looked up at the sky and felt Jenny stiffen beside him.

A band of gray light crept across the horizon. It was almost sunrise.

"My parents," Jenny squeaked.

"Aunt Gertrudis," Micah whispered.

"The bikes!" they both shouted at the same time.

They pedaled like they were being chased by a whole army of white tigers, but it wasn't enough. By the time they reached Micah's house, the sun had stained the sky an early morning pink.

Jenny didn't even stop. She shouted, "Bye! Good luck!" and streaked away with the Pooch Prowler rattling crazily behind her. Micah jumped off his bike and left it lying in the yard. He had one hand clutched tightly around Rosebud's pot of medicine.

I'm going to need good luck, he thought. He could only hope that Aunt Gertrudis hadn't woken up yet.

He made it up the stairs. He moved as quickly as he

could without letting the floorboards creak beneath his feet. The house was completely quiet. When he reached the door of his bedroom, Micah paused for a few seconds to catch his breath.

That was his mistake.

Just before he could turn the handle, Aunt Gertrudis stepped out of the guest room. Her eyes narrowed into slits as she took in his appearance. He was sweaty from the bike ride. He smelled like the menagerie animals and Rosebud's herbs.

Aunt Gertrudis had never been stupid. Her nostrils flared. "Where have you been?"

Micah knew he was a goner.

26

OLD LIES

Micah didn't tell her the truth. He said he'd been out riding his bike "for exercise." Aunt Gertrudis didn't buy it for a second.

At first, she only lectured, but then she saw the bootlace wrapped around Micah's wrist. Something Micah hadn't expected flitted across her face—recognition. An angry flush reddened her cheeks.

"Take it off," she said in a low voice. "Take that filthy thing off."

Micah shoved his hand in his pocket to hide it.

"Ephraim's old lies," she hissed. "I won't have it anymore! That thing should be *burned*." She swooped down on him and yanked his hand toward her.

"Let go!" Micah struggled to pull his arm free.

"It's a stupid, stupid joke," she said. "And it's dangerous."

"No it's not!"

She dug at the lace, but the more she pulled, the more it tightened around Micah's wrist.

Micah didn't know *what* had possessed her. "Stop it, Aunt Gertrudis. It's *mine*."

He snatched his arm as hard as he could and wrenched himself free.

Aunt Gertrudis stood crouched, her hand curled around thin air where his wrist had been a moment before. Slowly, she straightened. "Take it off."

Micah looked down at the bootlace. The knot he had tied yesterday stared innocently back up at him. He set his jaw and looked his aunt in the eyes. "I won't."

She made a disgusted sound in the back of her throat. "You've turned out just like Ephraim. I should have taken you away from him years ago." She glared a moment longer, then turned toward the staircase.

"He's not a liar, Aunt Gertrudis," Micah said to her retreating back. He wasn't sure where he'd found the courage. "Circus Mirandus is real. I've been there."

"You're grounded," she said without looking at him. She reached up with one hand to smooth the back of her bun. "If you won't take that thing off yourself, I'll cut it off. This foolishness will die with my brother. I won't have it infecting my life in Arizona."

Micah stared after her. "Then you'd better not take
me back to Arizona with you," he whispered. He was
surprised to realize that he meant it.

After he changed into his school clothes, Micah headed
downstairs to the kitchen. Aunt Gertrudis was in the
living room, and she didn't even ask what he was doing
in there. Maybe their latest fight had been good for something after all.

He put on the kettle to heat the water, then set Rosebud's
pot of medicine on the counter and pulled out its cork. He
sniffed. It smelled weird but not bad, like flowers and bacon.
He pulled the biggest mug he could find out of the cabinet and
dumped all of the powder into it. When the kettle was hot, he
let the bird sing for as long as he dared with his aunt nearby.

He carried the mug of finished tea carefully upstairs and slipped into his grandfather's room. Grandpa
Ephraim was asleep, and he looked worse than ever. His
skin was like paper, and he seemed to be fighting for every
breath even in his sleep. The sound was terrifying. *Blub
glub, wheeeeze.*

Micah bent down and kissed his cheek. "Wake up," he
whispered.

Grandpa Ephraim's eyes opened slowly.

"Micah." His voice was exhausted. "How did it go?"

Micah hesitated. He wanted to tell him the truth, to ask
him questions, but he looked so awful. "It was okay," he
said. "I'll tell you after school."

Grandpa Ephraim frowned.

"I made you tea." Micah helped Grandpa Ephraim prop himself higher on the pillows.

"I'm tired of tea," his grandfather wheezed.

"It's not Aunt Gertrudis's," Micah said. "It's special. From Rosebud."

Grandpa Ephraim's eyes widened. He took a sip from the mug.

"Is it good?"

His grandfather nodded.

"Drink it all," said Micah. "It's supposed to make you feel better."

Please, he thought, *let it make you feel better.*

The morning passed quickly, probably because Micah fell asleep while Mrs. Stark taught the class their new list of spelling words. He didn't have a chance to talk to Jenny until lunchtime.

"I was lucky," she said as she picked all of the pepperonis off her slice of pizza. "My parents were making coffee when I got home, so I sneaked in the back door, and they never noticed."

"My aunt noticed."

Jenny's eyes got huge. "No way. What did she do to you?"

"She grounded me." Micah had never been grounded before. It didn't bother him as much as Aunt Gertrudis's reaction to the bootlace had. She had seemed almost scared.

He looked down at it. It was a comforting weight against his wrist.

"Well, that ruins our plan," said Jenny.

Micah shoved a pepperoni in his mouth and swallowed it without chewing. "What plan?"

"To get the Lightbender to cure your grandfather, of course!" she said.

"You believe he can now?" Micah asked. It was strange for her to be the one convincing him that magic was the answer to his problems.

"If he's centuries old, then *something* has to be keeping him alive." Her voice was firm. "I'm coming up with a really good argument to convince him. I think we went about it the wrong way last night, but I'm sure that if we try again . . ."

Micah nodded slowly. The Lightbender had said he couldn't save Grandpa Ephraim. Micah didn't want to think he was the kind of person who would tell a lie that awful, but Jenny was right. Everyone at Circus Mirandus *was* very old.

That meant that there was still a chance. He couldn't give up yet. Hopefully, Rosebud's tea had bought him some more time.

27

ROSEBUD'S MITE

Grandpa Ephraim and Micah had always kept the house pretty clean, so Micah didn't know how Aunt Gertrudis had found so many disgusting chores for him to do that afternoon. Maybe she had her own evil version of magical powers. Within two hours of arriving home, he had scrubbed both toilets, scraped gunk out of the windowsills, and scoured a lot of burned stuff off the oven walls.

The only thing that made it bearable was the fact that Grandpa Ephraim was sleeping like a log. Micah thought his breathing seemed easier, and his face looked less pale. He was still snoring when Aunt Gertrudis told Micah to go to his bedroom.

Maybe Rosebud's potion is working, he thought while he pulled on his pajamas. *Maybe a mite of help will be enough.*

When he crawled into bed, his eyelids were already so heavy they felt like they had weights attached. He could barely remember the last time he'd actually slept the whole night. He had just let his head fall onto his pillow, which was a million times more fluffy than it had ever been before, when he heard the shout from his grandfather's room.

He was out of his bed and down the hall in a single motion, his heart slamming into his ribs. Aunt Gertrudis stood outside Grandpa Ephraim's door. She held a hand over her chest as she stared into the room.

Micah shoved past her.

Grandpa Ephraim was standing up. He was *standing* in front of his mirror, wearing his best suit and tying his necktie.

Micah froze, but only for a second.

"Oof!" his grandfather said when Micah grabbed him around the middle and pressed his face into his stomach.

"You're better," Micah said. They were the best words he'd ever said. "You're really better! I missed you so much."

Grandpa Ephraim laughed, and it was a real laugh instead of a coughing, choking one. He picked Micah right up off the floor and kissed his forehead.

"Isn't it amazing? I woke up and decided I felt good enough to stand, and once I did, I felt good enough to get dressed, and now," he said as he set Micah back down and patted himself all over, "I'm right as rain."

Aunt Gertrudis was still staring and clutching at her chest. "Ephraim!" she gasped. "It's not possible. You're dying."

Grandpa Ephraim winked at her. "I do know it, Gertie, but if I feel well enough to be up and about I'm going to take advantage of it."

He clapped Micah on the back. "Let's get out of the house. We have to celebrate the fact that my dying has been postponed."

This made Aunt Gertrudis come back to herself. "He's grounded, Ephraim," she said. "For sneaking out last night."

Micah didn't care about being grounded. He didn't care about how exhausted he'd been a moment ago. He didn't care about anything but the fact that Grandpa Ephraim was here, and he was healthy. Rosebud had done it. Her potion had worked. Micah's head couldn't take it all in, but his heart could. It wanted to climb right out of him and crow.

Grandpa Ephraim looked down at him. "I'm ungrounding you, Micah. It's very inconvenient for me if you're grounded right now. Put on some shoes. We'll go to a movie."

"A movie! Ephraim, you can't be serious."

"Do you want to come, too, Gertie?"

"No," said Micah.

"No! I don't want to come. You should get back in bed. You could relapse! I don't understand what's going on here, but we need to call the doctor."

Micah said, "It's magic."

"Don't be an idiot," Aunt Gertrudis spat.

Grandpa Ephraim reached out and hugged her. She stood as stiff as a post. "It really is magic," he said. "Are you sure you won't come with us?"

When they left the house, she was on the phone with Dr. Simon, trying to explain that Grandpa Ephraim was both dying and going to the movies against his doctor's orders.

Micah was too shocked and delighted to speak for most of the drive to the theater, but when Grandpa Ephraim pulled the car into the parking lot and started to unbuckle his seat belt, he found his voice.

"Wait."

His grandfather looked at him.

"Circus Mirandus. The Lightbender—he said he couldn't . . ."

His grandfather pressed his fingers gently to Micah's lips. "Not yet," he said. "I know a great deal, and you'll tell me the rest later. I don't know how long Rosebud's wonderful potion will last, but I want to enjoy every minute of it with you."

"But your miracle—"

"It will take care of itself at this point," Grandpa Ephraim said. "Forget about it please, Micah. For just a little while."

Micah didn't quite forget, but he did let his grandfather's enthusiasm carry him away for most of the evening. He had never been to a late movie before, and he had certainly never been to one wearing his pajamas with his tennis shoes. Grandpa Ephraim told knock-knock jokes while they waited in line. When they reached the box office, they didn't recognize any of the movies that were playing, so they bought tickets for the one that had the funniest poster. They ate popcorn and malted-milk balls and shared the biggest orange soda the theater sold. It was so big that they couldn't finish it in one movie.

So they stayed for another.

After the theater closed, they tiptoed crazily back to the car because they were trying to see who could avoid the most cracks in the pavement. When they climbed in, Grandpa Ephraim smiled at Micah. "Sleepy yet?"

"Not even a little." He would never be sleepy again if it meant that this night could last forever.

They went to a place that had putt-putt golf 24/7. They didn't keep score. They never did when they played games together. That way, when the game was over, they could agree that they had tied.

On the drive back home, Grandpa Ephraim turned the radio up loud, and they sang along to all the songs they knew. When his grandfather tried to make up the lyrics to the songs they didn't know, Micah laughed so hard that he started snorting.

It was so perfect, so magical, that Micah almost believed it would last forever. How could something so right ever stop? Then they pulled into the driveway, and Grandpa Ephraim coughed. Just once.

He shut off the radio and sighed. "I think that might be our cue."

"Everyone coughs once in a while," Micah said in a small voice.

"Maybe so," Grandpa Ephraim said. "But I think it's your turn. You have your own Circus Mirandus story to tell now."

"It's not as good as yours."

His grandfather smiled at him. "Maybe it's not over yet."

When Micah finished describing his trip to Circus Mirandus, Grandpa Ephraim had tears in his eyes. At first, Micah thought he was crying because he was disappointed, but then he wiped his face and said, "Oh, Micah, I remember. I'm so glad you've seen it. Wasn't it beautiful?"

He reached over for a hug, and Micah returned it as hard as he could. "But I haven't convinced the Lightbender to help you yet. You're going to . . . to leave me."

Grandpa Ephraim shook his head. "I'm afraid that you were asking too much of the Lightbender, Micah. I already told him what I wanted for my miracle, the second time he sent his parrot to see me. I never expected him to pull me back from death's door."

"I don't understand," said Micah. "What did you want from him? What did you ask for?"

His grandfather looked at him seriously. "For something very important and very difficult. For something stranger and more magnificent than anything he'd done before."

"What?"

"That's not something I can tell you yet. The Light-bender is still trying to make it happen. It's something that he can't do all by himself, you see."

Micah didn't see at all. What could possibly be more important than making sure that Grandpa Ephraim didn't die? "We could go to the circus," he said suddenly. The idea was so simple. He didn't know why he hadn't thought of it before. "We could ask Rosebud for more medicine. For gallons of it!"

But Grandpa Ephraim shook his head again. "I like to think," he said slowly, "that I could go one more time to Circus Mirandus. I like to think I have kept myself open enough to magic for that. But even if I can, I don't want to."

"Why not?"

Grandpa Ephraim was staring out the car window as if he could see something more beyond the glass than their ordinary street. He coughed again. "Because when you try too hard to hold on to something, you break it." He opened the door and motioned for Micah to do the same. "Sometimes, we need to let go so that other people can have their chance at the magic."

They decided to spend the last few hours of the night in the tree house they had built together.

Grandpa Ephraim laughed when he sat on half of a squashed tuna sandwich. "What's this?" he asked as he pulled it out from under him.

"Jenny and I must have left it."

Even in the dark, Micah could tell his grandfather's eyes were sparkling with interest. "Jenny," he said. "Your new friend. I wish I could meet her."

"You can," Micah said. "She'll visit if I ask. Tomorrow even. I know she will."

His grandfather didn't say anything.

Micah tried to push away the memory of how Grandpa Ephraim had been before Rosebud's potion, but it wouldn't let go of him. "You have to meet Jenny," he said. "We could call her right now."

"Good gracious, Micah! At this hour?" Grandpa Ephraim's voice was amused. "I doubt her parents would appreciate that."

"I . . ." Micah was at a loss. Then, he had a flash of inspiration. "Do you have any string?"

Grandpa Ephraim tipped his head to the side. "You're still wearing my bootlace."

Micah looked down at his wrist. "I know how you can meet Jenny," he said. The lace that Aunt Gertrudis had tried so hard to pry off that morning came away in his hand with a single tug.

He didn't worry about whether or not it would work. It was for Grandpa Ephraim, so it had to work. The knot began to take shape under his fingers. Here was a curve for how smart Jenny was, and there was a twist for their argument in the craft supply closet. Here a loop for the late night ride to Circus Mirandus, there another for the way Jenny pulled her braids when she was upset. Micah tied and tied, and when he was finished, he saw that he'd made exactly what he wanted.

He held it out to his grandfather. "This is Jenny."

Grandpa Ephraim cradled the knot in the palm of his hand. He closed his eyes and ran his fingers over it. When he opened them again, he was smiling. "Micah," he said, "do you know what you've done?"

"It's supposed to be like Jenny."

Grandpa Ephraim nodded. "It is. Your friend is truly one of a kind. You'd better take good care of her." He looked back down at the knot. "I have never seen anything like this in all my days. You've put memories into a bit of leather. Don't you see how remarkable that is?"

Micah shrugged. "You can tie knots, too."

"Not like this." Grandpa Ephraim reached out to Micah's wrist and carefully looped the bootlace around it. He turned Jenny's knot so that it was against Micah's pulse and tied the lace firmly into place. "This is something very special."

"I'm not special," said Micah.

"Don't you want to be?"

Micah thought about it for a minute. "Doesn't everybody?"

Grandpa Ephraim chuckled. "I suppose. But some of us aren't brave enough to find our specialness, and some of us make mistakes along the way."

He looked up at the stars through the oak's branches. "I'm glad you asked the Lightbender about Victoria. I never knew her whole story."

Micah frowned. Something about Victoria's tale had been bothering him. "I don't get how you married someone like the Bird Woman. How did you even meet her?"

"There's one story I never told you," his grandfather said. "It didn't have a happy ending, so I thought it was best to keep it to myself."

"I thought you'd told me everything."

"I told you everything about my first trip to Circus Mirandus."

Micah's eyes widened, and his grandfather nodded.

"When I was a young man, I tried to go back."

28

EPHRAIM AND THE BIRD WOMAN

No one at Circus Mirandus knew the part of Ephraim's story that he revealed to Micah that night in the tree house. How could anyone have suspected such an astounding coincidence? The day Victoria fell, the day she left the circus forever—on that very same day, Ephraim Tuttle was trying to find it.

His father had survived the war, and the Tuttles had spent a few blissful years getting on with their lives. Gertrudis had been born a happy, squalling baby, and the family had moved into a larger house in a better part of town. Ephraim had gone back to school and had even managed to stay long enough to graduate.

But life can be unkind. When he was nineteen, Ephraim's

mother died of a sudden illness, and after his father fell into grief, Ephraim found himself responsible for his seven-year-old sister. He handled the situation with a great deal of fortitude for his age. He didn't let it derail his plans. He was finally ready to ask the Lightbender for his miracle.

Ephraim had been searching for news of the circus for several months, and the investigation had become something of a personal quest. He spent a great deal of time listening to the gossip of children at the local park and visiting every traveling carnival and fair that he could find. It never occurred to him that something as simple as a letter might gain anyone's attention.

Eventually, he heard a rumor that the circus had been seen near Chicago. He packed his sister up and made his way there, certain that he had finally tracked them down. He was right to be confident. He was only a few miles away from his goal.

Ephraim pulled his sister up onto his back to jump across a dirty stream that ran right down the center of the woodblock street. The day was miserably hot, and Gertie stuck to Ephraim's sweaty back like she'd been glued there. He didn't mind. Finally, after so long, he could hear the music.

"And *you're* going to be a magician?" Gertie asked for the third time that afternoon. "You'll do tricks with your knots in front of hundreds of people?"

"I will," said Ephraim. "If they'll have me. I'm going to ask the Lightbender to teach me magic properly."

"I bet he doesn't have to teach you anything at all. Your knots are the best magic there is."

"You only think that because you haven't seen any other kind yet." Ephraim had an inkling, just the faintest idea, of what he could be with proper training. Knots were such a versatile thing really, especially once you started thinking beyond string. They were everywhere you looked and in many places that you didn't, and then there were knots that were completely invisible, like the ones that held families together.

He shifted her on his back. "We're almost there," he said. "I can feel it."

Then he turned a corner and found himself face-to-face with the Amazing Amazonian Bird Woman.

Ephraim had no way of knowing that Victoria had just left Circus Mirandus for good. He had no way of knowing how angry she was with the Lightbender.

"Good gracious!" Ephraim exclaimed. "You're the Amazing Amazonian Bird Woman."

She stopped dead. "I prefer Victoria." She looked him up and down. "Who are you?"

"Ephraim Tuttle," he said. "And this is Gertie."

Gertie peeked over the top of her brother's shoulder. "We're going to a magic circus," she chirped. "My brother's going to be a magician."

To Ephraim, the hot day suddenly felt twenty degrees warmer. The Bird Woman, who he had once thought was the most beautiful woman in the world, was twice as pretty as he remembered.

"I'm just going to ask if they can help me learn," he said. "I know a few things. Tricks. But the Lightbender, I mean the Man Who Bends Light of course, offered me a miracle."

"Oh *did* he?" said Victoria. Her eyes narrowed. "He doesn't do that often."

"I'm hoping instead of a regular miracle, so to speak, he might agree to teach me," Ephraim babbled.

"He must have seen a lot of potential in you." Her voice was contemplative. "He must have thought you had something special to contribute."

"Well, I'm not sure I would call what I do special—"

"Nonsense." Victoria smiled then, and to Ephraim it was like the sunrise. "So you're going to Circus Mirandus to meet the Man Who Bends Light. You're going to learn to be a . . . what is it you do exactly?"

Ephraim carried his old bootlace with him everywhere. He showed Victoria the knot he had tied for the Lightbender years before.

"How wonderful!" she said when he was finished. "That is just the kind of magic we're looking for at Circus Mirandus."

"Really?" Ephraim asked. "I've always worried that it was too little a thing."

"Really," said Victoria. She fluttered her eyelashes at him. "Surely you're not going right now, though?"

Ephraim was still staring at her eyelashes.

"We are," Gertie said.

"Oh dear!" Victoria shook her head. "I'm taking a short vacation from it all, myself. It would have been nice to have some company." She bit her lower lip. "I don't suppose you want to come with me."

"We don't," Gertie told her.

"You can always join Circus Mirandus later." Victoria laughed merrily. "Why, it's been around for thousands of years! I doubt we have to worry about it disbanding."

Ephraim was sure he hadn't been so lucky since Fish swam into his boot. "Of course," he said.

Victoria held her arm out, and Ephraim shook off his stupor. He set his sister on the ground and took Victoria's arm to help her across the street.

"But, Ephi!"

Victoria bent down to her. "It's not such a tragedy, darling," she whispered. "You would have been terribly disappointed in the end."

By the time Ephraim realized that Victoria had misled him, he was already very much in love with her. When she begged him to forgive her, he did.

"But I want you to understand that I'm going to keep looking for it," he told her. "I belong at Circus Mirandus. Sometimes I think I always have."

"Of course," she said. "I'm so sorry. Really, I am. I *do* love you. We could be a great team, you and I."

He believed her, and they were married soon after.

Ephraim found a job as a shoe salesman. It was supposed to be a temporary position, but money was in short supply. Gertie was growing up so quickly. She always seemed to need new stockings or shirts or skirts. Ephraim looked up one day to discover that his sister was eleven years old, and he was farther away from Circus Mirandus than he ever had been.

He could hardly let his wife and his little sister starve while he chased the circus all over the world. So, he stacked boxes of shoes and measured feet and dreamed of pipes and drums.

For her part, Victoria seemed content enough. She kept the house in order and directed Sunday choir, and if she was difficult to get along with now and then . . . well, at least Gertie had come to adore her. Once or twice, Ephraim caught his wife looking out the window at the birds with a calculating expression on her face, but he dismissed it as something he had imagined.

Then came the day when he spotted her hovering a few inches above the living room carpet. Victoria was staring out the window again, but this time she looked pleased.

"Your magic is back!" Ephraim was delighted. She had told him that she had lost her magic because of an accident. She didn't like to talk about it, and he didn't blame her. He couldn't imagine how hard it must have been for her. "This changes everything."

"Yes," said Victoria. "It certainly does."

She ran a slender finger down the glass pane. "Ephraim," she said, "have I ever told you about the other magicians? The ones who don't work for Mirandus Head, I mean. They might be very interested in meeting us, you know."

"That's good, I guess," Ephraim said.

"It is good, Ephraim. I'm talented. *You're* talented enough, though of course you need some training to reach your full potential. It's a thought, isn't it?"

"But Victoria—Circus Mirandus. It's waiting out there for both of us now. For *all* of us."

"Mmm, yes," Victoria said. "Gertie's still eager for the place, isn't she? It won't be easy to take her along if she's outgrown the idea, though, will it? The manager does tend to be *selective*."

"You know she's still dying to see it! And I can't wait to tell her about your magic."

Victoria stepped over to kiss him on the cheek. She smiled. "I can't wait either."

One Saturday not long after that, while her brother was at work, Gertrudis Tuttle was lying on the front porch of the house when Victoria came out to sweep. Gertie had her tongue between her teeth, and she was staring intently at something in her hands.

"What have you got there, darling?" Victoria asked.

"It's *the* bootlace. I don't know why it won't work for me. Ephraim does it like it's nothing."

Victoria laughed. "Oh, Gertie, that's a good one! I didn't know you still believed your brother's old stories."

"Of course I do."

Victoria rolled her eyes. "Do you really think his silly knot hobby is magic?"

"Yes. I've seen him do it. He's going to be a great magician one day."

"Honestly, sweetie, you're smarter than that. He says I can fly!"

Gertie looked up at her calmly. "You can. I don't know why you never do it, but Ephi wouldn't lie to me."

There was a strange glint in Victoria's eye. "He did," she said. "Think about it. If I could fly, I wouldn't be sweeping this porch. I would be doing, oh I don't know, a hundred other things."

"But—"

"*Think,*" said Victoria. "If I could do magic, if anyone with any sense could do magic, would they really squander their time putting on shows for children?"

"Ephraim says they do. It sounds nice."

Victoria leaned against the railing. "It sounds foolish. *Real* magicians would be powerful people. They would be rich and famous. They would control *entire countries*. If Circus Mirandus existed, it wouldn't be a good thing. It would be a huge waste of talent. That's not the sort of place you should believe in."

"Ephi wouldn't lie," Gertie repeated.

Victoria set down her broom. She spread her arms wide. "If magic is real," she said, "prove it."

Gertie squinted at her. "How would I do that?"

Victoria shrugged. "I'm sure I have no idea. If Ephraim's stories were real, I suppose you could jump off something tall, and I could fly up to catch you before you hit the ground."

It wasn't that Gertrudis was stupid. She just had an inordinate amount of faith in her brother to tell the truth and in Victoria to keep her safe.

She coiled the bootlace neatly and put it aside. She used the porch's banister to climb up onto the roof.

"You're going to be sorry," said Victoria.

Gertie stood on the sharp edge of the tin roof and stared down. "I don't know why you're testing me like this. I really do believe in magic. I know you'll catch me."

Ephraim came home just in time to see his sister leap.

Victoria didn't catch her.

She didn't even try.

29

THE WRONG ANSWER

The tree house was quiet for a long while after Grandpa Ephraim finished his story.

"It was only a broken arm," he said eventually. "It could have been much worse for poor Gertie. But I'm sure you understand why I had to ask Victoria to leave."

Micah privately thought that his grandfather should have had Victoria arrested.

"I woke up one morning a few months later to find your father screaming his head off on my front stoop. Only a few days old, mind you, and not a stitch of clothing on him. He was wrapped in a bath towel. If she hadn't tucked a white feather in with him, I might not have known who he was."

Possibly, Micah thought, *Victoria was the kind of person they didn't even want in prison.*

"I never found out what happened to her after that. To be honest, I didn't want to know. I don't think Victoria ever understood love. Not really." Grandpa Ephraim coughed. "I *am* glad I married her."

"Why?"

"I'm glad because she gave me your father."

"Oh." Micah looked up through the branches of the tree. A couple of stars winked at him. "I don't remember him as well as I should. Or mom. What they were like, I mean. I mostly remember how they looked. Sometimes, I worry I'll forget that, too."

His grandfather squeezed him around the shoulders in a one-armed hug. "Well, they were splendid people, if I do say so myself. And they gave me the best grandson in the whole world."

When Grandpa Ephraim said things like that, Micah almost believed they were true.

They stayed up together to wait for the sunrise, even though the coughing was getting worse. "Your miracle?" Micah had to ask just one more time.

"I'm waiting for an answer. I hope I'll have it soon."

It took them a long time to climb down the tree house's rope ladder. When he got to the bottom, Grandpa Ephraim had to hunch over his knees to catch his breath. When he stood up, he said, "Thank you for sharing this night with me."

"It was the best I've ever had," Micah said. Even as he

said it, he was afraid that there would never be another one like it.

"It's the best I've had," his grandfather replied, "since I was ten years old."

Grandpa Ephraim shook his head when he saw Dr. Simon's car was parked on the street out front. Aunt Gertrudis must have insisted that he come over. Right before they walked in the door, Micah's grandfather looked down at him.

"I do wish you and your friend had talked the Lightbender into coming for a visit," he said. "It would have been something to see him standing in my very own house."

"I don't think he would fit in," Micah replied as they stepped into the living room.

Grandpa Ephraim chuckled; the *blub glub* had come back. "That's the whole point of him," he said. "That's the whole point of it all."

Then he sat down on the sofa and started to wheeze.

It didn't stop.

Grandpa Ephraim's eyes were closed, his chest was heaving up and down, but he didn't seem to be getting enough air. Then a horrible rattling sound joined the blubbing, glubbing, and wheezing.

Micah wasn't quite sure what happened next, but he thought he must have called for help because Aunt Gertrudis appeared at the foot of the stairs. "Stop caterwauling."

Dr. Simon, looking startled, was behind her. He ran to

Grandpa Ephraim and checked his pulse. Then he swore and started pulling things out of the duffel bag he always brought with him when he made house calls. He only paused for long enough to point at Micah and say, "Get him out of here, Ms. Tuttle."

Aunt Gertrudis took Micah to the kitchen. "You'll stay right here if you know what's good for you," she said before she left.

He sat down at the table and stared at the daisy-patterned tablecloth for a hundred years. When Dr. Simon finally came into the room, he knelt beside Micah.

"Now, Micah," he said, "I know we haven't talked about this much, but you're a smart young man and I know you can understand."

"Is he gone?" Micah whispered.

Dr. Simon sighed. "Your grandfather is still with us, but you need to realize that it's only going to be for a very little while. Okay?"

"Okay," Micah said. Even though it wasn't. Even though it never would be.

"Your great-aunt and I are going to bring his things down from upstairs and try to make him comfortable right here on the sofa. We're going to do everything we can, but he doesn't have much longer. The rest of the day at the most. You understand?"

"Okay," Micah said. He couldn't find another word.

Aunt Gertrudis appeared. She looked at Micah almost as if she wanted to say something, but she didn't. She and the doctor headed upstairs to bring down Grandpa Ephraim's bedding and his breathing machine.

Micah went into the living room to sit with his grandfather, but he stopped in the doorway. "Chintzy? What are you doing here?"

The parrot had just flown through the open front door. "I want to state for the record that it wasn't my decision to make!" she squawked. She landed on the back of the sofa and stared sideways at Grandpa Ephraim. "Is he asleep?"

"Do you have a message?" Micah asked.

Chintzy shifted from foot to foot. "I have an answer."

"I'm awake."

Grandpa Ephraim's voice was so weak that Micah wasn't sure he'd actually said it until his eyes opened. He hurried forward and crouched beside the sofa.

"Answer?" Grandpa Ephraim gasped.

Chintzy's feathers puffed. "No." She took off without another word.

"No." Grandpa Ephraim stared at the ceiling.

"What's 'no' the answer to?" Micah asked.

"It's the *wrong* answer," he said. "They're wrong." It was hard to tell because of how he was breathing, but Micah thought he sounded angry.

Grandpa Ephraim reached out then and clutched at the front of Micah's pajama shirt. "You have to go," he said. "Circus Mirandus. Now."

Micah shook his head. "I can't leave you. Doctor Simon said . . ."

He trailed off. His grandfather's eyes were clear and so very serious.

"Go," he wheezed. "Bring him back. Lightbender. Miracle." He released Micah's shirt. "'No' is the wrong answer."

The kitchen telephone hung on the wall next to the refrigerator. Jenny's phone number was as easy to remember as she had said it would be.

A woman, who must have been her mother, answered. "I'm afraid Jenny's getting ready for school," she said. She had a faint accent. "I can have her call you back if you like."

"It's an emergency."

"What kind of emergency?" her voice was concerned.

"Homework."

"Oh. I'll get her for you."

Micah thought it said a lot about Jenny's family that homework was considered a valid emergency.

A minute later, someone yawned into the telephone. "Micah? What's wrong?"

"We have to get the Lightbender to come as soon as possible. This morning. You have a plan, right? Can you come with me?"

"*Now?* What about school? My parents won't let me skip."

"Just pretend like you're going to school, and don't get on the bus."

"Micah," Jenny said. "I can't. My mom drives me."

Micah couldn't think fast enough. He needed Jenny with her advice and her plans. "Well *try*, okay? Meet me there."

He hung up the phone before she could answer. Dr. Simon and Aunt Gertrudis were on their way down the stairs. They would see him leaving if he ran out the front door.

So he climbed out the kitchen window.

30

A REALLY BIG GORILLA

Mirandus Head had suspected from the beginning that the answer to Ephraim's final request wouldn't be the one he'd hoped for. He had come to Peal to appease the Man Who Bends Light and to see if there was any outstanding reason to change his mind.

It hadn't been easy for him to refuse. He had watched Micah carefully during his visit to the circus. He had liked the boy right away, just as he had Ephraim, and in his own way, he was sympathetic to their plight. But his first responsibility was always to Circus Mirandus. He couldn't afford to make emotional decisions.

The answer was no.

The manager thought that Micah would accept that. He felt sure that he had the boy's measure. With the difficult decision made, he turned his thoughts to other matters, and Circus Mirandus went back to business as usual.

As if anything could be usual when Micah Tuttle's grandfather had given him a mission.

Circus Mirandus was every bit as beautiful in the daylight, but there seemed to be fewer people around, maybe because of school. Other than Micah, only two children waited in front of Geoffrey's stand to have their tickets examined. Neither of them was Jenny. Micah knew it wasn't fair to expect her, but he was so surprised not to see her that he realized he must have been counting on her even more than he'd thought.

Geoffrey let the other children in. He squinted at Micah through his monocle, looking just as alert as he had last time. Micah wondered when he slept.

"Ticket?" Geoffrey asked, as though he had never seen Micah before that moment.

"I'm Micah Tuttle. I have an invitation."

"Oh, an invitation," he said. "Let's see it then."

Micah frowned at him. "You saw it just the other night. Don't you remember?"

Geoffrey drew himself up to his full height and pointed at the entrance sign over his head. "I've been here since the very beginnin'," he announced. "The very beginnin'. And I remember everythin'."

"Right," said Micah. He didn't have time for this. "So I can go in?"

"If you have a ticket." Geoffrey had a bored look on his face, but there was something in his eyes that was paying close attention to Micah.

Micah stared at the tents. They were so close. "Was the invitation only good for one night?"

Geoffrey scowled so that his monocle looked like it was cutting into his eyebrow. "The invitation is good for as long as Mr. Head wants it to be," he said. "And Mr. Head doesn't want it to be anymore."

No. Micah's stomach dropped all the way to the soles of his feet. "I *need* to come in. I'll apologize to Mr. Head. I'll do anything you want."

The ticket taker looked unimpressed, and Micah suddenly knew that he wasn't the first person who had begged. How many people must have tried, over thousands of years, to be let in once their tickets had expired? How many had succeeded?

"More've tried than you can imagine," Geoffrey said, as though Micah had asked the question out loud. He switched his monocle to the other eye. "And none get one minute more than they're given. That's my job."

He pointed again at the sign over his head. "And I've got a perfect record."

A teenage girl holding a jack-o'-lantern appeared behind

Micah. Geoffrey didn't even blink. "Two hours," he said without looking at her.

To Micah, he said, "No ticket, no entry."

Micah shook his head stubbornly and stepped forward. Before he could take a second step he heard a low growl. Something white flashed at the corner of his eye.

Bibi.

Micah backed away, but the growling didn't stop. It got louder. Micah kept walking.

The invisible tiger didn't go quiet until he reached the edge of the recreation complex. There, he stopped to think. Knowing that nobody had made it past Geoffrey and Bibi since 500 B.C. was the opposite of encouraging. On any other day, Micah might have given up, but this wasn't any other day.

He looked around for inspiration. There had to be something that would turn all of the noes into yeses. There had to be a way to make things right, if only he could find it.

And he did.

Micah had three things that none of those other people trying to break into Circus Mirandus had ever had— orders from Grandpa Ephraim, Jenny Mendoza for a friend, and a really big gorilla.

It shouldn't have been easy for a kid to steal a giant gorilla balloon in broad daylight, but to Micah's surprise, getting to the big ape was simple. It wasn't as if the park had full-time balloon guards. Micah ignored the locked gate and climbed right over the short fence onto the ball field.

In the sunshine, the balloons looked much less myste-rious. He checked the knots that held the gorilla's ropes to metal stakes in the ground. They weren't secure by Tuttle standards. So the problem wasn't getting the balloon; the problem was attaching himself to the balloon. Micah didn't want to be stuck floating through the air for hours, but he also didn't want to fall.

He thought about Bibi's fangs and shivered. *Grandpa Ephraim's counting on me,* he reminded himself. *I have to risk it.*

It took several minutes to undo three of the four ropes, and Micah's hands were sweaty with nerves. The gorilla had tipped onto its side in the air overhead, and it would be pretty noticeable even from a distance.

Micah took the laces out of his tennis shoes. Not long enough, but maybe . . . He took off his pajama shirt and rolled it into a long tube. He wrapped it around his chest and tied it, using a shoelace to secure the ends with the strongest knot he knew. Now he had his own pajama harness. Well, actually it was more like a pajama sash, but Micah decided that thinking of it as a harness made it feel safer. He attached the harness to the gorilla's final tether and bent to unknot the rope from its stake.

It was tighter than the others had been. Micah jammed his finger while he was loosening it, but it came undone for him just like the others had. For an instant, he was excited that he'd done what he'd set out to do. Then, his pajama

harness caught him under the armpits and yanked him off
the ground. He yelped and clamped his eyes shut.

Micah stretched his toes down and felt nothing. The
wind was at his back. *It's okay,* he told himself. *You can do
this for Grandpa Ephraim.*

He forced himself to look around only to discover that
things weren't going quite the way he had expected. He
had thought he would be up a lot higher and moving a lot
faster. The gorilla was so big. He'd assumed they would
rocket toward space together and toward Circus Mirandus, and at just the right moment, Micah would let go so
that he could land in the circus and not go splat.

It sounded ridiculous, now that he reconsidered it.

Since wind always blew toward Circus Mirandus, he
was going the right way. The problem was that he was
only about eight feet off the ground, and even though he
was rising steadily, it didn't seem to be happening quickly
enough. At this rate, Bibi would eat him from the ankles up.

He held on to his harness with both arms as he and the
gorilla drifted over a chain-link fence. *All right, Micah,* he
thought. *There are a couple of things you can do now.*

Should he hang on and hope for the best? Or let go?
He probably wouldn't hurt himself too badly from this
height, and he could try to get into the circus some more
normal way. His shoulders were already aching. He decided
to let go.

Unfortunately, it had taken him quite a while to decide,
and when he looked down to see what he would be landing

on, Micah realized that eight feet had turned into fifteen feet. Now, letting go seemed like a very bad idea. The wind picked up speed, and Micah gripped his harness tighter.

He lost a shoe as he sailed over the bleachers beside one of the soccer fields. He stared down at it. It was *tiny*. He drifted higher and higher, until the sight of the ground made him dizzy and he had to look up at the balloon. He tried to swallow his nerves, but his mouth was so dry that they got caught in his throat.

It was the music spiraling up that finally made him look down again. He was passing right over the ticket stand now, and the little man that was Geoffrey never glanced skyward.

Micah soared over Circus Mirandus. He couldn't see the faces of the people below him, but they were obviously all having a wonderful time. The children were running from tent to tent. Performers were turning somersaults. He was so far away from them and so worried for Grandpa Ephraim and so sure that he had just made the biggest mistake ever by tying himself to a space-bound gorilla. He felt like he was part of a different species.

It's okay, he told himself. *You've got a plan.*

The plan was for Micah to let go of the harness when he was right over the center of Mr. Head's menagerie. He would fall through the roof of the tent and land in the giant fish tank. He was fairly sure that Grandpa Ephraim's fish wouldn't attack him. He would splash down in all that water, and he wouldn't even be hurt.

Jenny had said an aerial assault on Circus Mirandus would work. Micah trusted her judgment.

But for some reason, when the time came, Micah couldn't let go. His arms were cramping, and he passed by Mr. Head's tent a lot more quickly than he had planned to. He was so high up that it definitely wasn't safe. Probably Bibi could fly anyway, and the manager just hadn't mentioned it. Excuses ran through his mind as he watched the scarlet fabric of the big tent pass beneath his feet.

He floated over Rosebud's wagon.

That was it, he realized. *That was my one and only chance, and I missed it.*

He knew then, as surely as he had ever known anything, that he was going to die. He was going to die just like all of the other stupid kids who had tried to break into Circus Mirandus probably had. The tiger would use his bones for toothpicks. His eyes stung and blurred. He could barely make out the next tent.

It was black fabric covered with golden suns.

It's too far down. I can't.

Bring back the Lightbender, Grandpa Ephraim had said. *No is the wrong answer,* he'd said.

But Micah still didn't know what the question was.

It was one of the hardest things he'd ever done, but he reached up with one shaking hand. He touched the knot that held his harness together *just so.* And he fell.

It was so quick that Micah didn't even have time to scream. He hit taut fabric, and pain shot through him like a lightning bolt. He heard a loud *rrriiiiipp,* and he kept falling. He fell right through a burst of fireworks, through a wheel of colored light, and he crashed down onto something that was hard and soft at the same time.

It shouted, and it smelled like a long leather coat that had seen a hundred adventures.

Micah wondered if he was dead. His head felt like it was enormous and full of boiling water. His back throbbed. Someone had definitely stabbed him in the shoulder with a knife.

Yes, he decided. *Being dead feels like this.*

But then the Lightbender was there, crouching over him. His face was white, except for a streak of blood under his nose, and he reached out with his long fingers to brush Micah's hair away from his face.

Micah slowly realized that the Lightbender's mouth was moving. That meant he must be speaking to someone, but he wasn't making any sound. For some reason, this was funny, and Micah laughed. Only laughing filled his chest with sharp points, so he had to stop right away.

He tried to look around. The whole tent was full of light, plain yellow light, and the stands around Micah were filled with kids. Why did they all look so frightened?

The Lightbender glanced away for a second, and Micah saw him open his mouth wide as if he was calling somebody. The Strongman appeared, his bowler hat askew, and then Micah was rising up into the air.

"Nooo," he moaned, and the Strongman froze.

"Oh," Micah said. The Strongman was the one picking him up. It wasn't the giant balloon. "You're okay."

The Strongman still didn't move. He looked almost as afraid as the children in the stands.

The Lightbender stared into Micah's eyes, and Micah remembered. "You have to come," he said. "Grandpa Ephraim. You gave him the wrong answer."

The Lightbender's mouth moved again, and Micah was tired of him not making any noise now, because he needed to know what he was saying. He tried to focus on the Lightbender's lips, and finally, like it was coming from miles away and underwater, he heard ". . . anything . . . be still . . . Rosebud . . ." and then, ". . . what you've done to yourself."

Aha. He's wondering how I broke into the circus.

"Gorilla," Micah explained.

Then he passed out.

31

THE SIDE EFFECT

When Micah woke, his face was pressed into something warm and gray and hay-smelling, and he felt seasick. He realized that whatever he was on was moving with a sort of swaying, thumping motion, so that might have been why. Or it could have been the taste in his mouth, which was like he had licked all of the shower drains in the United States of America. Being still and quiet seemed like a good idea. Going back to sleep seemed like an even better one. He closed his eyes.

Then, he heard a soft voice say, "McDonald's again. We've already passed this. Are you quite sure you know where you're going, Jean?"

That voice belonged to the Lightbender. Micah had to get him for Grandpa Ephraim! He sat up fast, and it made the seasickness much worse.

"Steady," said the Lightbender, and one leather-covered arm grabbed Micah around the chest to keep him from falling.

"You have to come," Micah said as soon as his stomach stopped trying to crawl out of his mouth. Then he looked around, and he saw his own hometown from the back of the world's most intelligent elephant. The Lightbender was pointing with one finger toward the McDonald's restaurant a few blocks away from Micah's house.

"I am trying to do as you ask, Micah," he said, "but I'm afraid that Jean's infallible sense of direction may have failed her."

Big Jean trumpeted and waved her trunk in the air.

"No," Micah said. "We're really close."

"Are we? I feel as if I am traveling in circles. We keep passing Mr. McDonald's building."

Micah was sitting in front of the Lightbender on an elephant. Everything felt less than real. "It's a restaurant," he said. "There's more than one. They look a lot alike."

Jean made a huffing noise, as if to say, "See, I told you." She ignored a red light, looked both ways, then crossed the street.

"You're coming," Micah said. "You're coming to see Grandpa Ephraim." He leaned forward to hug the parts of Jean he could reach, but he was wearing some kind of long, green velvet jacket over his pajama pants. His arms were trapped in sleeves that were much too big.

"How could I refuse?" the Lightbender said drily. "I have seen and done many surprising things during my life, but I have never had a child fall out of the sky during one of my shows."

"It hurt," Micah said. "I won't do it again."

His arm tightened for a moment, pulling Micah closer. "I do hope not. You nearly died."

Micah looked up at him to tell him that it wasn't that bad, that he was fine, but the Lightbender's eyes were as gray as a storm cloud. He also had dried blood under his nose. "We are very fortunate that Rosebud is a genius with her potions," he said. "She wanted me to tell you that you are not a duck, but a little boy, and that you cannot fly."

"I had to get to you. Geoffrey wouldn't let me in, and I didn't want Bibi to eat me."

The Lightbender chuckled. "Bibi wouldn't have eaten you, Micah. Nobody at the circus, whether man or beast, would ever hurt you or any other child." His smile faded. "At least not on purpose."

Big Jean trundled past a day-care center, and even though a lot of little kids were playing in the sandboxes outside, none of them noticed the elephant. It made Micah feel like he was watching the world pass by through a window.

"What do they see when they look over here?" he asked.

The Lightbender looked toward the day care. "Nothing

at all. It's the same trick I use to hide the circus from those who aren't called."

"Is Mr. Head mad that you left?"

The Lightbender tipped his head to the side. "I am not a prisoner at Circus Mirandus, Micah. I am allowed to come and go as I choose. But, more often than not, I choose to stay because the circus needs me. It is difficult for me to keep it hidden when I am away. I lose focus, and distance is a problem."

"I'm glad he wasn't mad."

"Oh, he was furious," the Lightbender said mildly. "But not because I left. He was angry because you were hurt, and because you broke through all of his clever protections, and because we are having a serious disagreement at the moment."

"What do you mean?"

The Lightbender was quiet for such a long time that Micah thought he might not answer, but then he sighed. "I promised Ephraim Tuttle a miracle. Anything within my power."

"I know." Micah tried not to sound accusing, but he wasn't sure he had managed it.

"It's something we all do from time to time." He was gazing off into the distance, and Micah knew he wasn't staring at the jet trails in the clouds or the city water tower. "When we meet a child who is particularly . . . receptive. Circus Mirandus exists to nurture magic, to keep it alive in the world beyond our gates. I make the offer less frequently than the others. It has never seemed fair to me to single one person out of the crowd for a treat, but Ephraim was different. So I promised."

The Lightbender laughed, at himself Micah thought. "He saved it," he said. "Through all these years, over the course of however many small tragedies life has thrown at him, Ephraim never called in his miracle."

Micah frowned. "Is that strange?"

"Children usually ask for things that aren't miracles at all. They want special shows, souvenirs. Extra tickets. Their own pet giraffes. Such little things."

"That seems wasteful."

The Lightbender shook his head. "You say that because you have lived the sort of life in which you could have used real miracles. I am sorry for that. Ephraim was the same."

Big Jean turned onto Micah's street.

"I thought," the Lightbender said, "that Ephraim would ask me to bring his father home safely from the war. It was the obvious request. It was something he wanted very much."

"Why didn't he?"

"I've never been sure. I was ready to do it. It wouldn't have been easy, but it would certainly have been manageable for someone with my skills. A few illusions in the right places . . . But Ephraim asked to keep his miracle in reserve, for a time when it was really needed, and since I had already promised, I agreed."

The Lightbender smiled at Micah. "Your grandfather

grew from a very wise boy into a very wise man. When he contacted me, I knew that whatever he had decided to ask for would be difficult."

Micah couldn't help himself. "He didn't ask you to cure him?"

The Lightbender didn't say anything.

"It's just that you've lived for so long!"

"Ah. So that's why you have such faith in my ability to conquer death." He looked troubled. "I didn't realize how it must seem to you. I am afraid I am sometimes out of touch with . . ."

"Ordinary people?"

The Lightbender shook his head. "You are not ordinary."

Micah wasn't sure whether that was a compliment or not.

"My extended life span is a side effect, Micah. It's not the result of some potion or spell I could share with Ephraim."

"A side effect of your magic?"

"A side effect of Mr. Head."

He saw the expression on Micah's face. "I am not teasing you. Though he has a way with animals, Mr. Head isn't what you would consider a magician. He isn't even what you would consider human. His gift is powerful but passive. Living things under his care thrive. Circus Mirandus is under his care, and I am part of Circus Mirandus."

"He's not human?" He had looked human enough to Micah. "What is he then?"

"He is the manager. He has always been the manager."

"Wait. Are you—"

"I am as human as you are, Micah. All of the performers are. It's only Mr. Head who is . . . unique."

Micah struggled with this idea. "So he's kind of like the circus's battery?"

"That's right." The Lightbender sounded amused. "Mr. Head is a battery."

Big Jean stopped in front of Micah's mailbox. The street was quiet. Dr. Simon's car was gone.

"So what *did* Grandpa Ephraim ask you for?"

"Something private for now." The Lightbender glanced away. "I'm still not sure I can do it. Much depends on other people, particularly Mr. Head, and he has already refused once. But Ephraim asked only that I try, so I will."

32

LETTING GO

· F I S H ·

The Lightbender asked to meet with Grandpa Ephraim alone. At first, Micah wanted to refuse, but then he realized his grandfather and the Lightbender were about to see each other face-to-face for the first time in years. Maybe that moment would mean more for both of them if Micah didn't butt in.

He took a deep breath. "Okay," he said. "I'll stay with Big Jean."

The elephant snorffled the top of Micah's head with her trunk, so at least one of them was pleased.

The Lightbender frowned. "Not for long," he said. "I just need a moment with your grandfather in private, and then I will call you in."

"Sometimes it's hard to wake him up."

"I know," he said. "Rosebud has given me something that will help."

"I hope so." Micah knew it was time for the big warning. "There's also my aunt."

"Chintzy mentioned her." He didn't look worried, so Micah was sure Chintzy hadn't mentioned Aunt Gertrudis thoroughly enough. "I'll make sure she stays out of the way."

The Lightbender looked to the elephant. "Jean, guard."

She snapped, as fast as an elephant could snap, to attention and saluted him with her trunk. The Lightbender tugged his leather coat down in the front, which didn't change how he looked one bit as far as Micah could tell, and then he strode up the path to the front door and let himself in without knocking.

As soon as the Lightbender had disappeared, Big Jean tromped right over to the garden hose on the side of the house and picked it up with her trunk.

"Are you thirsty?" Micah asked. She *had* walked an awfully long way this morning.

He turned on the hose, thinking he would give her a drink, and soon, he was spraying her all over. She even knelt down on her front legs so that he could get the top of her head. Before he knew it, Micah was wet from his big green velvet coat to his bare toes.

He thought he was doing it all to help her, but when the Lightbender poked his head out the front door and called for Micah to come inside, he realized that he'd lost track of time. Since he had started washing Big Jean, he hadn't worried about what might be happening in the house.

He patted her trunk. "Thank you."

She nudged him toward the door.

In the living room, Grandpa Ephraim was lying on the sofa with his eyes open. Micah could hear his lungs, the same *blub glub* as usual, but he looked better than he had that morning. He was still sick, but he mostly looked tired. And happy.

"Micah," he said in a voice that was stronger than Micah was expecting. "You've grown."

Micah sat down on the floor beside him and kissed his cheek. "I don't think I could have," he said. "I didn't go to school today."

His grandfather nodded. "And you've grown more than ever."

For a time they just sat there. Micah held his grandfather's hand on top of his blanket, and Grandpa Ephraim smiled. The Lightbender stood out of the way in the corner next to the television. Aunt Gertrudis was nowhere to be seen.

"I won't tell you that you shouldn't have done it," Grandpa Ephraim said at last, and Micah guessed that the Lightbender must have told him about his adventure with the gorilla balloon. "Because it was a ridiculous, amazing thing to do, and once in a while, it's good to be ridiculous and amazing."

Grandpa Ephraim was always saying things that sounded so important Micah wanted to wrap them up in boxes and keep them forever. He tried to think of an important thing to tell him in return. "I love you," he said. It was the best he could do.

"And I love you. More than anything. So try to keep your feet on the ground in the future if you can."

His grip tightened, and Micah squeezed back.

"Thank you for bringing the Man Who Bends Light to my living room. Doesn't he look wonderfully out of place?"

Micah remembered what his grandfather had said just that morning. "That's the point of him."

They both looked at the Lightbender, whose eyebrows lifted in confusion.

"Two of the most wonderful people in my life in the same room," Grandpa Ephraim said. "I must be the luckiest old man that ever lived." He motioned to the Lightbender with his free hand, and the Lightbender came to squat beside Micah.

He took the frail wrinkled hand in his own smooth fist and held it gently.

"Now," murmured Grandpa Ephraim. "Let's be here together for as long as we have."

Micah squeezed his hand harder.

"For as long as we have," he said again. "Then, when the time comes, we'll all let go."

None of them said anything else. Micah wiped at his eyes with his free hand a few times, and Grandpa Ephraim's chest pulled itself up and down more and more slowly. The Lightbender didn't twitch; he didn't even blink. He stared at Ephraim Tuttle like all the secrets of the universe were written in the lines on his face, and maybe they were.

But Micah only saw his grandfather. When the *blub glub* finally stopped, it hurt even more than he had expected.

33

ELEPHANT SPEED

Micah didn't know how long he sat beside Grandpa Ephraim after it was over. It might have been hours. It only felt like a few minutes.

"His answer," Micah said eventually. "His miracle. Was it still a no?"

"It was not," the Lightbender said. "You changed it."

"To yes?"

"To it depends. But I am feeling rather confident."

He took Micah by the hand and led him out of the house. Big Jean was ruining the grass by rolling her gray bulk in the giant puddle that the garden hose had made in the front yard. She looked pleased with herself.

"Time to go, Jean," said the Lightbender.

Micah didn't realize that he was being taken along until the elephant hunched down in front of them, waiting for them to climb aboard. The Lightbender took his seat on top of Jean then pulled Micah up to sit in front of him. While they set off down the street, Micah tried to think of where he ought to be at that moment, if not on top of an elephant going past the local McDonald's.

Not with Grandpa Ephraim, because he was gone. Not at school, because you didn't go to school after you had just watched your grandfather die. *With Aunt Gertrudis,* he realized. She was his guardian now. He clung to Jean and wished that she would stomp slower, but she kept moving along at elephant speed.

This time, Micah heard the pipes and drums before he could even see the recreation fields. "Will the circus still be here through the weekend?"

"Most likely. That is the plan for now."

"It's just that I'll miss it when it's gone," Micah said. "Even if I'm not allowed in. I'll miss knowing the magic is there."

"We're always somewhere."

"It's not the same."

The Lightbender bowed his head. "I know."

Jean trumpeted when they were in sight of Circus Mirandus to let everyone know she was coming, and Micah tried to convince himself that saying good-bye wouldn't be so bad. They passed by the place where the giant balloons were tied. They swayed in a lonely sort of way, as though they missed the gorilla.

"Micah," said the Lightbender. "What do you think magic is?"

Micah could tell that the question was serious, so he tried to come up with a serious answer. He thought of everything he had seen at Circus Mirandus and everything Grandpa Ephraim had seen when he was a boy.

"I guess it's what's inside of people like you," he replied. "The parts of you that are too big to keep just to yourself." He paused. "Does that sound dumb?"

"It sounds wise," said the Lightbender, "and not too far from the truth."

Then he leaned forward and placed his hand on Micah's wrist. He hooked a long finger through the bootlace, and he whispered in Micah's ear. "*This* is magic. And I, of all people, am in a position to know."

The words spun in Micah's brain. He wasn't sure he believed them, but the Lightbender refused to look away. Slowly, Micah nodded.

"Remember that," the Lightbender said. "No matter where your life eventually takes you."

He didn't say anything else, and Micah realized he was waiting for a response. "I will."

The Lightbender dipped his head in acknowledgment. "Now, I must ask you for a rather large favor. I need to borrow that wonderful bootlace from you. I know how important it is to you, but I promise—"

Micah slipped the bootlace off his wrist and held it out to him. Jenny's knot was still as perfect as it had been when Micah tied it.

The Lightbender looked surprised.

"You came to see Grandpa Ephraim," Micah explained. "I trust you."

The Lightbender took the lace gingerly from him and examined it. "Thank you. This will be a great help to me. I will see it is returned to you very soon."

Then, Big Jean stopped moving and made a dangerous sound, a powerful rumble that sent shock waves up through Micah's bones.

The Lightbender's eyes widened. "Oh no. I've been away too long."

People were everywhere. *Grown-ups* were everywhere, with cameras and strollers and curious looks on their faces. A group of policemen were scratching their heads nearby, muttering about permits and city ordinances and animal control.

Geoffrey was swinging his monocle from its chain as though he might use it to fend off the half-dozen adults who were trying to force money into his hands. Mr. Head stood beside him, arms crossed over his chest. He had such a look of fury on his face that even the television crew from the local station was keeping its distance. Bibi was completely visible for a change, standing in front of the gate with her hackles raised.

Everywhere, people were on their cell phones. "We've

just got to bring the kids, David," Micah heard one woman say. "It doesn't look like much, just some traveling fair, but we haven't had an outing in ages."

Micah watched the fairy swarm flit past. They were flickering madly, as if they were struggling to stay out of their butterfly forms for more than a few seconds at a time. Micah hated everything about what he was seeing. These people didn't understand. They were trying to turn the circus into something *normal*.

"Can you fix it?" he asked. People were starting to press in around Big Jean. He didn't know what they saw, or how the Lightbender was keeping them at a safe distance, but Micah had the feeling that if he stopped the elephant might just stomp her way straight through the crowd to her tent. "You can fix it, can't you? I don't want them to hurt it."

"They can't hurt Circus Mirandus, Micah," the Lightbender said firmly. "Not really. This is just—"

"Horrible."

"Messy," said the Lightbender. "And sad."

"But fixable?"

"Of course. Now that I have returned we can take care of it quickly enough. Only . . ." He frowned at Micah.

"What?"

"I'm afraid I am going to be busy."

It took Micah a minute to understand. He swallowed hard. "It's . . . it's okay. I had to go back to Aunt Gertrudis sometime anyway."

"I suppose so," the Lightbender replied, but he kept

scanning the crowd. Suddenly his eyes narrowed. "Forward, Jean," he said, and she rumbled again.

People moved out of their way in a hurry. The police unhuddled and started directing everyone away from the elephant.

Micah looked on in surprise. "What are we?"

"A fire truck I think. One passed Jean on the way to your house before you regained consciousness. I noticed that all of the other vehicles moved over for it."

Micah was about to ask where they were going, since they weren't moving toward the entrance, but then he spotted two long black braids. "Jenny!"

His friend was holding on to the hand of a woman who must have been her mother. The woman was wearing a sweatshirt with a needle and thread logo on the back, and she looked frustrated.

"What do the men who fight fires wear in this century?" asked the Lightbender.

"Umm . . ." Micah had seen firefighters of course, but he didn't know what to call their outfits. "Yellow suits and helmets?"

"How odd."

Big Jean stopped a short distance from Jenny and her mom so that Micah and the Lightbender could dismount. When Jenny saw Micah, she pulled free from her mother and ran toward him. Her eyes were red, and her face was puffy.

"I tried, Micah," she said when she reached him. "I tried so hard to get here. I made myself sick so that they'd call

Mama to come pick me up from school, and then I made her drive by here twice. She couldn't see it at first, and she started to think I was *lying*, but then it appeared all of a sudden."

She grabbed Micah around the neck. "I'm sorry I didn't get here sooner."

"I'm sorry you're in trouble," Micah said when he could breathe again. "I got him to come."

She looked toward where the Lightbender was talking to her mother. "Why is he wearing that weird helmet? And driving a fire truck?"

"It's not a fire truck. It's Big Jean."

Jenny stared. Then she shrugged. "Magic is going to take some getting used to."

They didn't have time to talk more because Jenny's mother came to tell them that she was taking them home. "That has to be the strangest fireman I've ever met," she muttered. "He's asked me to let you stay with us until this evening, Micah. Something about a family emergency? Are you all right?"

He nodded, even though he wasn't sure it was possible to be all right in a world without his grandfather. He looked around for the Lightbender. He was striding through the crowd toward Mr. Head. People were already turning away from Circus Mirandus with disappointed expressions on their faces.

Micah didn't know what they saw.

He didn't want to.

34

PRACTICALLY CHEATING

As far as Mirandus Head was concerned, there had never been a more exasperating magical artifact than the Tuttle family bootlace. After borrowing it from Micah, the Man Who Bends Light passed it around Circus Mirandus. No, he *paraded* it around Circus Mirandus. He told everyone and anyone who would listen about how brave Micah Tuttle had nearly died trying to save his grandfather's life, and then he told them that only one thing stood in the way of Ephraim's miracle.

The manager.

By the end of the day, Mr. Head couldn't step out of his tent without hearing about Micah. As a matter of fact, he couldn't even step *into* his tent without hearing about Micah. He was, unfortunately, fluent in elephant. He soon felt like he was under siege in his own circus.

The Man Who Bends Light was wise enough to steer clear of him while he put his plan into effect, but he reappeared the next day when Mr. Head was making his rounds. He looked as smug as a cat in a creamery.

"Wasn't this a tad juvenile?" Mr. Head groaned when the magician joined him on his walk. "Couldn't we have spoken about the matter in private?"

"I wanted you to know I have the public's support."

"You neglected to tell me he was Victoria Starling's grandson."

The Man Who Bends Light didn't have the decency to look ashamed of himself. "Chintzy is as good at keeping secrets as usual, I see," he said. "Does it matter?"

The manager sighed. "You *know* it's not completely irrelevant. After her years here she may not have aged as quickly as a normal person. As far as we know she's still out there, scheming."

"Ephraim was a good person. Micah is a good person."

"I am aware of that."

"I want you to change your mind."

"Really?" Mr. Head grumped. "I had *no* idea."

They stopped walking when they reached the gates and looked back toward the tents. Circus Mirandus bustled, as it always did. It was a joyful place, a safe place, and ultimately, the manager was the one who was responsible for keeping it that way.

"Very well," he said at last. "But I have one condition."

Grandpa Ephraim's funeral wasn't a big event. The preacher said some nice things, and Aunt Gertrudis forced Micah to dress in a suit that itched. One of the ladies from the church tried to feed him a whole plate full of cucumber sandwiches.

Micah didn't pay much attention to the service. Grandpa Ephraim had left two days earlier, holding on to Micah's hand and the Lightbender's, and that was special. This was just a ceremony with the cheapest casket and the cheapest tombstone that Aunt Gertrudis could find.

It should have made Micah angry, because his grandfather deserved the best, but it didn't. Grandpa Ephraim thought cheap things were just as interesting as expensive ones.

Jenny's family came to the funeral. Her mother hugged Micah every time he came within reach, and her father pulled him aside to tell him how happy Jenny was to have made a friend at school and how sad they all were that he would be leaving. They both looked so scandalized when Aunt Gertrudis tried to drag Micah away from his grandfather's grave that she let Micah stay in the cemetery for as long as he wanted after the burial.

Things were changing too fast for Micah to keep up. Aunt Gertrudis had said he had one more week at school while she "finalized affairs," then they would move across the country to live in Arizona. Standing by Grandpa

Ephraim's grave, Jenny promised to call Micah on the phone all the time.

Aunt Gertrudis sniffed. "We can't afford the long-distance fees."

Jenny put her hands on her hips. "Micah," she said, even though she was looking at Aunt Gertrudis, "I will send you letters every week, and I'll include self-addressed stamped envelopes."

Even Aunt Gertrudis couldn't think of anything bad to say about that. She stared silently at Grandpa Ephraim's headstone for a minute, and then she went back to the car.

Jenny stood with Micah a while longer. They didn't say much. She wiped her eyes with a handkerchief. "I'm sorry for being terrible company."

"You're not."

But eventually Jenny's parents told her it was time to go.

"I'm so sorry we have to run, Micah," her mother said. "Arturo has a busy afternoon at the university, and I've got bridesmaids that need new sleeves. You will be fine, won't you?"

"I'm good," said Micah. "Thank you for coming."

"Of course. Now, if you need anything, please call." She shot a suspicious look at Aunt Gertrudis's car, but she didn't say more.

Micah watched them leave and tried not to feel lonely, but even Aunt Gertrudis was better than an empty cemetery.

He was turning to go when the *whoosh* of wings stopped him. Chintzy dropped out of the sky right over Micah's

head and fluttered down to Grandpa Ephraim's tombstone. She placed a familiar bootlace on top of it. "A perfect
landing!" she said. "Better take notes on how this flying
business works. Your family has a history of failure."

"Oh, *ha-ha*," said Micah, reaching for the lace. "Aren't
you clever?"

"I am."

Micah hadn't heard from the Lightbender since the day
Grandpa Ephraim died. And he knew better than to try
breaking into Circus Mirandus again.

Chintzy cocked her head sideways. "I've got a message
for you."

Micah nodded.

"'To: Micah Tuttle, From: The Lightbender,'" she said.

"He called himself the Lightbender?"

"Sometimes I edit for him." She fluffed her feathers.

"'Dear Micah,'" she squawked. "'I am sorry that we
parted as we did. I wish I could have been there for you
today, but the circus is moving to a new location soon and,
as you've seen, I'm needed.'"

Chintzy paused to scratch her head with one foot, and
then continued. "'Remember what I told you about magic.
You have more than a bit of it in yourself. Be careful not to
let it slip away from you, and you'll always be able to hear
the music. Whatever you choose to do with yourself, you
are a brave, clever young man, and I know you will go far
in life.'"

"End message," said Chintzy. "Would you like to hear the part he cut out?" she asked eagerly.

Micah frowned. "If he cut something out doesn't that mean he didn't want me to hear it?"

"He was trying to stick to Mr. Head's rules."

"Don't tell me. I don't want him to be in trouble with Mr. Head."

"It's about your grandfather's miracle."

"Tell me," said Micah.

Chintzy bobbed up and down. "It was a postscript. It said, 'Don't look down.'"

"That's it?"

"Good thing he took it out," Chintzy squawked. "A big fat hint like that. He was practically cheating."

35

ON THE WAY TO ARIZONA

Micah's last week at home wasn't a good one. The Lightbender's message begged to be deciphered, but Micah had never been much good at riddles. Jenny came up with a list full of ideas, each more unlikely than the last. She wasn't holding up well. Every time Micah mentioned his departure, she grew tearful.

"I promise I'll write," Micah said over lunch one day. "All the time. You'll probably get tired of me."

Jenny sniffled. "I always wanted a pen pal."

It took Micah several days to think of what he could do for Jenny. He wanted to thank her for all of her help. When he finally came up with an idea, he worried that

Jenny would think it was embarrassing, or just weird. But he wanted her to have something to remember him by, and he wanted her to have a little magic of her own.

"It's a bracelet," he blurted out as he handed her the newspaper-wrapped present on his last day of school.

"You're *supposed* to let me open it first." She tore into the newspaper and opened the box to find the knotted blue string inside.

"It's like my bootlace," said Micah. "Only the knot is like me instead of you." He felt his cheeks redden. "It's kind of a friendship bracelet. So we won't really be apart, no matter how far away Aunt Gertrudis takes me."

Jenny let Micah tie it around her wrist, and then she burst into tears.

"You don't like it?"

She hugged him so tightly that he almost strangled. "I d-don't want you to g-go," she sobbed. "You shouldn't have to go. Your aunt's awful."

Micah sighed and patted Jenny on the back. "It's okay. Really. It won't be forever."

She pulled away from him. "What do you mean?" She swiped at her eyes with the back of her hand.

"One day I won't have to live with Aunt Gertrudis anymore." He took a deep breath. He'd had the thought for a while, but he hadn't voiced it aloud. "One day I'm going to go back to Circus Mirandus. Like Grandpa Ephraim always wanted to. I'm going to find them even if I have to steal a hundred gorilla balloons."

Jenny looked surprised for a moment, but then she nodded. *"Good."*

Packing up for the move was depressing. Micah went through Grandpa Ephraim's belongings and selected things to sneak away from Aunt Gertrudis's going-to-the-dump pile. He hid his grandfather's necktie and the ticket stubs from the movies they had seen together the night before he died. He saved most of the photographs. He couldn't decide whether or not he wanted to keep the picture of Victoria, but in the end he didn't have to. One day it was simply gone.

Micah wasn't sure whether his aunt had packed it away or destroyed it. Part of him hoped it was the latter. Maybe getting back at Victoria, even in such a small way, would make her feel better. He couldn't ask. They hadn't spoken to each other, except for Aunt Gertrudis snapping a random order every now and then, since the day after the funeral.

They had been packing up the bookshelves in the living room when his aunt spotted the bootlace on his wrist. She left and returned a few seconds later with a pair of scissors. She slapped them onto the dusty shelf in front of Micah.

"Cut it off."

He saw her distorted reflection in the shiny metal of the scissors. Her lips had disappeared into a stern frown. "Don't you *want* magic to be real?" he asked as he turned to face her. "Maybe just a little bit?" If he could find even a shred of common ground with her, the next few years would be a lot easier.

But Grandpa Ephraim's Gertie was long gone, and Aunt Gertrudis looked at Micah like he had asked her if she wanted to contract a rare disease. "I want my life to go back to normal. I want to make the best of a bad situation. I *don't* want to cling to infantile fantasies. Cut it off."

Micah pushed the scissors aside. "I won't. Not ever."

He didn't know what had changed since their last argument over the bootlace. Maybe it was how he said, "I won't." He would have told her that two plus two equaled four in exactly the same way.

She took the scissors back to the kitchen and stopped speaking to him.

It was an improvement in some ways. They didn't argue anymore. But this new version of Aunt Gertrudis had given up on Micah, and she went about getting her life "back to normal" as though he wasn't even going to be a part of it. She didn't mention him in phone calls to her friends. She stopped asking him about school. Micah felt like a piece of furniture.

The trip to Arizona in Aunt Gertrudis's car was the longest Micah had ever been on, and they had only been driving for three hours. Even mute, she had a special way of making every mile last for an eternity. When she merged onto the interstate, the sun coming through the windshield turned the car into an oven.

"Do you mind if I turn on the air-conditioning?" Micah asked.

When she didn't answer, he turned the air-conditioning on.

Aunt Gertrudis turned it off.

It was the closest they had come to a conversation in days.

Furniture, he reminded himself. *Ugly furniture that she never wanted in the first place.*

He watched the other cars pass by. A little girl wearing a hat with bunny rabbit ears on it waved at him from a minivan. Micah waved back gloomily. He hoped the girl was going to wherever Circus Mirandus was. She would fit in there.

After a while, the other cars stopped passing them. Traffic crawled down the highway. When Aunt Gertrudis had to hit the brakes to avoid rear-ending the truck in front of them, she hissed like an angry old cat.

"People are so inconsiderate here."

Not long after that, traffic stopped completely. They were caught in a jam.

Micah watched the families in the cars around them while his aunt muttered under her breath. The car grew warmer and warmer in the sun, and his eyelids grew heavier and heavier. He let them fall shut. He was almost asleep, right on the edge of a thought that looked like it might be a dream, when he heard pipes.

And drums.

Micah jerked forward so quickly that his seat belt caught and yanked him back. He unbuckled it and whipped his head around. They were still stuck in the traffic jam. Some people were getting out of their cars and stretching. Others were climbing on top of their vehicles to look ahead toward where the problem must be.

"Ridiculous," Aunt Gertrudis grumbled.

Micah saw one of the climbers, a teenager in a T-shirt covered with skulls, point. He started to shout.

Micah reached for the handle of the car door.

"It's probably a wreck," said his aunt.

"No," said Micah. "I hear music. *The* music."

He got out of the car. When she didn't tell him to get back in, Micah hesitated. "Don't you want to see?" he asked her. "You could give it one more chance."

She looked at him. For a moment, Micah thought she was considering it, but then she turned away. She gripped the steering wheel like it was a life preserver.

Micah started walking. Aunt Gertrudis never called him back.

Micah passed minivans and tractor-trailers and cars, and he still couldn't see anything but traffic. But the music was getting louder. He started to jog toward it, then to run.

Please, oh please, he thought as his feet beat the pavement.

When he reached the cause of the traffic jam, he stopped dead.

"It was an earthquake, man," said a pale guy standing next to him. "It has to have been an earthquake."

Micah was too shocked to say anything at all. A chasm had been torn across the interstate and as far as he could see in either direction. It was so deep that it looked like it went to the center of the planet, and craggy rocks jutted from the walls. A Greyhound bus was so close to the edge that the asphalt under its front wheels was crumbling.

Across the gap, a hundred yards away, Micah could see other interstate travelers staring back at them. Everyone looked as amazed as he felt.

"Man," said the pale guy. "Dude, this is going to be all over the news. It's like the new Grand Canyon."

The music was still calling Micah from the other side of the chasm. He couldn't possibly reach it. He walked right up to the edge and stared down. It was so far it made him dizzy, so far that it should have been impossible. It reminded him of how much it had hurt to fall from the gorilla balloon, and he took a step back.

The drums pounded in his ears. The pipes filled the air. It was too cruel. Why would Circus Mirandus be calling him if following the music meant walking over the edge of a canyon?

Maybe, thought Micah. *Maybe I'm just imagining it.*

Was it possible to want something so much that you could hear it even when it wasn't there?

No, he decided. He knew he wasn't imagining the music. Circus Mirandus was out there somewhere beyond this cliff. The Lightbender was out there. Micah inched forward until the toes of his sneakers were over the edge. He could feel the empty underneath them.

His stomach clenched as though he'd already fallen. *Don't look down there,* he told himself. He started to take a step back, but then he paused.

"Don't look down," Micah said aloud. His voice echoed off the canyon's walls.

Micah knew this was one knot he couldn't untangle. Whatever he chose, he would be taking a huge risk. Stepping forward might mean falling to his death. Going back to Aunt Gertrudis might mean never seeing Circus Mirandus again.

Was it worth it?

Micah closed his eyes. He heard the pale guy shout, "Dude! That kid's gonna jump. Someone grab him!" But nobody did. Part of Micah waited for the ground to drop out from under him, but it never happened. He just kept moving forward with his eyes shut tight until the music stopped.

He listened. It was very quiet now. He couldn't hear the roar of people or cars. His chest started to ache. He hadn't even realized he'd been holding his breath. He let it out in one big gasp and opened his eyes.

In front of Micah was an almost-empty stretch of interstate. Almost empty, because a man in a long leather coat stood in the center of it beside an elephant. The Lightbender spread his arms wide and smiled.

"Hello, Micah," he said. "How do you like my miracle?"

36

MIRACLE

Grandpa Ephraim had never wanted the Lightbender
to save him. He hadn't wanted to use his miracle for
himself, but for Micah. The Lightbender explained everything as they rode Big Jean toward an EXIT sign.

Grandpa Ephraim's last wish was for Micah to have the
chance that he himself had lost. He had asked the Lightbender to teach him to use his magic; he had asked him to
take Micah to Circus Mirandus.

"I don't think you can imagine how shocked I was," the
Lightbender said. He was holding Micah close, as if he was
afraid he might lose track of him if he let go. "I have spent my
life making magic for children, but I have never tried to teach

a child before. I have certainly never tried to raise one."

"You're doing fine so far," said Micah. He was almost breathless with happiness. "You're doing more than fine."

He couldn't believe that this was really happening. He was going to live with the Lightbender. He was going to learn magic. Grandpa Ephraim could have asked for anything for himself, and instead, he gave Micah everything.

"Yes, well," the Lightbender sounded a little embarrassed. "I have not had the job for very long. I assure you that I will make plenty of mistakes in due course."

"And Mr. Head?" Micah asked. "He really doesn't mind?"

"He was . . . reluctant to risk welcoming someone so young and untried into our ranks."

"Because of what my grandmother did."

The Lightbender didn't disagree. "He wanted me to make absolutely sure that you loved Circus Mirandus as much as we do."

Micah realized then that the canyon across the interstate had been a test. "That cliff," he said.

"Some of my better work," said the Lightbender. "Did you like it?"

"Um . . ." said Micah. "Remind me not to make you angry. Ever."

The Lightbender was still laughing when a familiar red-feathered blur plummeted out of the clear blue sky. Chintzy landed on top of Jean's head and dropped an envelope into Micah's lap. He looked at the return address.

It was from Jenny.

"Do you know what that girl is going to do to my work-load?" the parrot huffed. "You've been living with us for *ten minutes.*"

Micah ripped it open, and a letter fell out along with a self-addressed, stamped envelope. He was surprised to see that Jenny's handwriting was even sloppier than his own.

> *Dear Micah,*
> *Welcome to Arizona! My mom is letting me*
> *send this letter next-day mail so that it*
> *will be waiting for you when you arrive. I*
> *hope the trip with your aunt wasn't too*
> *bad.*
>
> *I know you just left, but I already miss*
> *you. Thank you so much for my bracelet.*
> *It really does make me feel like you're not*
> *so far away.*
>
> *I've been doing some research on Arizona.*
> *I made a list of fun facts for you about the*
> *state. Daddy says we might have time to*
> *vacation this summer, and I'm trying to*
> *convince him that the desert will be more*
> *educational than Florida.*
>
> *I need to get this letter in the mail,*

so I'd better go now. Please write back.
Your friend,
Jenny Mendoza
    P.S. Holy smokes! Chintzy!
    I don't even know how she got in my
room, but she told me that the Lightbender
has some kind of test for you and that you're
going to pass because she's given you a hint
and that she'll deliver your mail from now
on. Holy smokes, Micah! Are you really
going to live at Circus Mirandus? Write back
NOW.

"You have a wonderful friend in her, Micah," said the Lightbender.

"The best," Micah agreed. He touched the bootlace at his wrist. "I know we'll probably be traveling all over the place, but is there any way I can visit her sometime?"

"This is how it starts," Chintzy warned the Lightbender. "Next he'll be asking you for a pony."

"I will work something out with Mr. Head," said the Lightbender. "Children don't usually visit Circus Mirandus more than once, but then again, we don't usually have a child living there."

He raised an eyebrow at Chintzy. "And he can have a pony if he really wants one. We have plenty of them."

Micah reread Jenny's letter while Chintzy bickered with the Lightbender. He couldn't believe how very *good* his life was going to be. Big Jean stomped along at elephant speed, but Micah knew they would catch up with Circus Mirandus eventually. And when they arrived, he wouldn't have to worry about tickets or being invited in.

You never need an invitation to go home.

ACKNOWLEDGMENTS

When I wrote the first draft of *Circus Mirandus*, I was alone with my words and my imagination and my prayers. But the first draft was a mighty tangle. This page is for the magicians who helped me unravel it.

My sister, Kate Beasley, read it first and last and a hundred times (no, really) in between. She is a marvelous writer with her own stories to tell, but she always finds the time. Kate, you are my favorite. We go together like toast and cheese.

Susan Fletcher, Martine Leavitt, and Uma Krishnaswami are three of the smartest, most generous people I have ever met. They all left their marks on the manuscript while I was studying at VCFA.

Elena Giovinazzo is *that* agent. She can fix your novel and explain the publishing industry and assuage all your fears with a single phone call. I adore her, and the rest of the Pippin Properties family, forever.

My editor, Namrata Tripathi, is the perfect guide. She is brilliant, and she makes me want to be a better writer. I am so grateful to her for believing in *Circus Mirandus*. She and the team at Dial are exceptional in every way.

And, of course, I want to offer an elaborate and lengthy thank you to the readers. But I'd better not. Life is short, and wonderful stories are waiting for you.

Go find them.

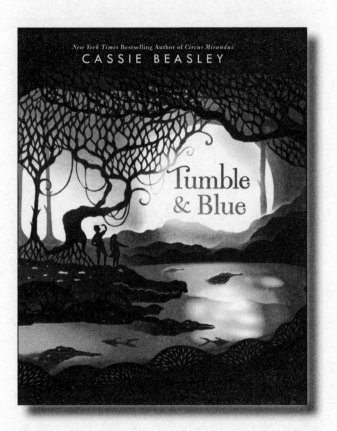

From time to time, I bother to notice them.

Tourists. They come reeking of their bug repellents and their sunscreens, and the *clicker-snap* of their cameras nibbles away at the song of the swamp until I wonder if they can hear it at all.

In my memory, the humans who traveled the Okefenokee were a different sort. These new ones are less afraid. More curious. And, on the whole, they are quite a bit plumper.

It would be a lie to say I have not felt the stirrings of temptation. Especially in the deep summer, when the sun glazes them with sweat so that they glisten, juicy and bright as silver fish.

Scrumptious, but I resist. My business with mankind is not, strictly speaking, that of the predator.

I do have to remind myself of that when they come carrying maps. How they love those little guides with their safe paths through the swamp, all dotted out and color-coded. Acres of prairie and blackwater and cypress and pine captured as lines on bits of paper. Made small as gnats.

Such arrogant morsels, you humans. That's something that hasn't changed.

Which brings me to the beginning, to a couple of humans long dead but still causing trouble for their descendants. Almira LaFayette, Walcott Montgomery—names from a story that is only now approaching its end.

It's been two hundred years, and I still remember the taste of them on the night air. Thick, greedy, sweet with desperation. When they met on the edge of the swamp, the red sickle moon was cutting a hole in the black of the sky.

My moon.

And in its bloody light those two bad people were looking for an easy way out of the messes they'd made. Montgomery was a horse thief. LaFayette was a murderous young bride. He had robbed a militiaman, and she had shot her husband in the gut with a revolver three days after the wedding.

Why?

Perhaps they had their reasons. I didn't care to ask. What matters is that they ran from justice and toward me, and they reached my island at the same time.

Precisely the same time. An irksome situation for me and a tricky one for them.

I offer only one change of fate. Only one chance at a new future. Those are the rules, and they can be terribly sharp when broken.

Well. At least they didn't use maps to find me. Even Montgomery and LaFayette knew that much.

Creatures like me don't fit in between a cartographer's lines.

Creatures like me . . .

We can only be found in the places where maps dare not go.

ONE

BLUE

B lue Montgomery almost missed the sign. Kudzu was vining up its wooden posts, and its paint had begun to peel. It looked more like part of the wilderness around it than something made by human hands.

But his dad seemed to know where the turn was even in the dark. He steered the truck off the asphalt and onto dirt, and in the shine of the headlights, Blue had just enough time to read, WELCOME TO MURKY BRANCH, GA. and, POPULATION: 339.

"'Bout two miles to your granny's house from here!" Alan Montgomery raised his voice over the rumble of the washboard road. "I used to run from our front door all the way out to the sign. Back when I was your age. I could make it in under twelve minutes. Not bad at all."

He drummed his fingers on the steering wheel and gunned the truck's engine.

Blue watched the woods speed by. His dad had been like this ever since they'd left the hotel in Atlanta. Talky. Casual. As if he didn't know that every mile marker they passed stung Blue like a wasp.

There were no more mile markers out here, though. No cell phone reception either. Most of the world had no idea that Murky Branch existed.

The road curved, and through a break in the pines, Blue saw the house. Three stories of ghostly white paint and wraparound porches were illuminated by a moon that was close to full.

"Your granny's going to be so glad to see you," said his dad. "She's been nagging me to bring you around for forever."

He whipped the truck onto the gravel driveway just as the glowing numbers on the dashboard clock changed to read midnight. Rocks flew up to ping against the doors. Blue winced, imagining the scratches and dings in the new paint, but he didn't say anything.

His dad had taken a break from racing last year, but now that he was planning to get back on the track, he only had one speed. Fast.

The truck passed an old chicken coop that was cooping a mower instead of chickens, then a shed with a roll of rusting barbed wire propped against one wall. Blue caught a glimpse of the huge garden beside the house. It was filled with tomato cages, silver pinwheels, and chin-high corn.

His dad dodged a sprinkler, bounced the truck over a coiled hose, and stopped inches from the trunk of a giant pecan tree. "Well," he said, letting go of the wheel, "the place hasn't changed much. You need help getting the—?"

"I've got it," Blue muttered, opening his own door.

Blue's right arm had been in a cast for weeks. He'd tried to stand up to a bully at school and, in hindsight, that hadn't been the best idea. Fighting usually wasn't when you were literally destined to lose.

But the arm would be fine. Sometimes, when the itching let up, Blue forgot that he was wearing the cast at all.

He reached into the truck's backseat, but his dad was already there, stretching to grab the overstuffed duffel bag. "Let me take that for you, Skeeter."

He set off toward the house, and Blue followed, dragging his feet.

The sounds were strange. In Atlanta, even at night, sirens and horns had screamed past the hotel where they'd been living, but here, the darkness was loud with chirring insects and frog song. Blue felt like his ears had been tuned to the wrong channel.

He reached the edge of the porch's wide cement steps and looked up. He had a vague memory of the Montgomery house from when he was a little kid. But it was eerie now and unfamiliar.

Carved over the front door's lintel was a scene that had been painted over so many times the finer details were obscured. Two figures, a man and a woman, were shaking hands under a crescent moon.

The columns that supported the porches were carved as well, some of them into cranes with raised beaks and others into alligators standing on the tips of their tails. The gator nearest Blue had had one of its eyes drilled out. It looked like someone had gouged the creature's soul right out of the socket.

Blue climbed the steps and took in the rest of the porch. A pair of worn-out athletic shoes, dirty with grass clippings, had been left beside the mat. The door had a scuffed bottom and etched windows on either side. He couldn't see through the filmy curtains, but he figured everyone in the house must be asleep.

Thunk.

Blue turned. His dad had dropped the duffel bag onto the porch boards. He was rocking back and forth on his heels like he always did after a long drive.

When he caught Blue's stare, he stopped. "What?"

"Nothing."

Blue bent to pick up the bag with his good hand. He tried to lift it onto his shoulder in one smooth motion, though its weight made his arm burn. He thought he'd managed pretty well, but even in the dark, he could see the way the corners of his dad's eyes creased.

"It's not that heavy," Blue said. "I bet I'm as tough as any of the other cursed Montgomerys."

His dad was looking everywhere but at him. "We've talked about this," he said. "I'm not expecting you to get involved when . . . *if* it happens the way they say it will. You're only here to visit your granny while I work some things out. The timing's a coincidence is all."

Blue wished he would stop lying.

The red moon only appeared once every hundred years. According to family legends, on that night one person could travel into the swamp and claim a great new fate. And when you were cursed—as Blue and half of the other Montgomerys were—a new fate was worth the risk. It couldn't be an accident that his dad had decided to leave him here this summer, when the moon was due to rise again.

"Well," his dad said, scuffing his feet against the mat, "go on in. Your granny hasn't locked a door in seventy years."

"Aren't you going to come in with me? To say hello to everyone?"

His dad just stood there, tall and silent. He was sandy-haired, like Blue, but lately it seemed that was the only thing they had in common. Alan was one of the lucky Montgomerys. One of the gifted ones. He had a talent for winning, and as a racer, he'd been unbeatable.

Blue, on the other hand, couldn't even win a game of tic-tac-toe.

"Nah," his dad said at last. "I've got to be gettin' on."

Blue wondered if they were going to hug each other

good-bye. He kind of wanted to, even though none of this was fair. He took a step forward.

His dad turned away. "Got to be gettin' on," he said again. He stomped down the stairs and paused at the bottom to look back over his shoulder. "Tell your granny I said hello. And your cousins."

"Yessir."

"Don't pay too much attention to anything your granny might say about me. And whatever you do, *don't* tell her I'm taking up racing again. She's got this way of looking at things . . . well, it's soft, that's what, and lord knows you don't need more of that."

Blue stiffened.

His dad was scraping one of his shoes against the patchy grass. "Bye."

Blue didn't reply.

Alan strode back to the pickup. Blue had picked the color. Golden brown. He could see the flecks of glitter in the paint even in the dark.

Blue cleared his throat. "I'll see you soon, right?" he called. "You'll be back by the end of the summer?"

The truck door opened with a *clonk*, and his dad pulled

himself up into the high leather seat. "Just take care of yourself."

"Yes, sir."

But they were supposed to take care of each other.

The door slammed. Blue lifted his cast in a wave, but he was too late. The truck had already taken off across the cluttered yard. Its headlights illuminated the green plastic mailbox at the end of the driveway, and then it was gone.

Blue was alone on the porch of a house he only half remembered, on a night full of sounds that were all wrong.

He stared up at the carving over the door. Once upon a long time ago, one of Blue's ancestors had won the great fate for himself under the red sickle moon. Walcott Montgomery had gone into the Okefenokee Swamp a poor man on the run from his enemies, and he had come out of it different. Luckier.

Wealth, health, long life—Walcott had had it all. And he'd changed the fortunes of every Montgomery who came after him.

If you believed the stories, it wasn't entirely Walcott's

fault that half of the family had ended up cursed. The woman in the carving—Almira LaFayette—had been there, too. She'd made it to the hidden island at the heart of the swamp at the same time as Walcott. They'd fought.

Things had gone wrong.

But it would be someone else's turn this time. And if Blue could be that someone . . .

How, though? Other Montgomerys would be descending on Murky Branch. He assumed it would mostly be the cursed relatives. The famous actors, millionaires, and geniuses didn't need to show up, did they?

But even though the Mongomerys who came might have their own terrible fates to contend with, none of them were born to lose. Spelling bees, video games, hide-and-seek—it didn't matter how simple the competition. Blue couldn't win.

His arm itched and ached inside its cast, and as he scratched at the plaster, he realized how tired he was of being himself.

He looked around the empty porch, and the dirty athletic shoes beside the door pulled at his eyes. None of his own shoes were great for running. He'd only ever been a spectator, and running shoes were for racers. Weren't they?

Weren't they for people like his dad, who was probably halfway back to the highway by now, driving like he was about to cross yet another finish line?

Driving away from Blue.

Thunk.

Blue let the duffel bag fall hard. He kicked off his flip-flops. He stomped over to the shoes.

Racing shoes, he thought. *Not-for-Blue shoes.*

And when he stuffed his bare feet inside of the shoes, they fit. Like they had been waiting for him.

Like they were ready to try something new.